IT HAD TO BE YOU

Deborah Simmons

Published by Bennett Street Books

Book Layout © 2016 BookDesignTemplates.com

Cover Design by Tugboat Design

CHAPTER ONE

The bride was having a meltdown.

It had not reached reality show levels yet, but Paige was not about to stand by and watch when she knew how quickly things could go south. Or even more south. Although the young woman in a diaphanous gown and veil might resemble an angel, she was shrieking like a banshee while brandishing the four-inch heel that had once been attached to her strappy sandals.

Wading through the horror-stricken bridesmaids who gathered around feeding the frenzy, Paige made her way to her client.

"Don't panic," she said as she wrested the stiletto from the young woman's fierce grip. "What about your backup shoes?"

Paige was a firm believer in backup shoes, simply because so many brides chose really uncomfortable ones for the ceremony. Afterward, most were more than happy to don a less painful pair.

"I can't wear those!" the bride practically screamed.

Okay, so that was not an option. "Where did you get these?" Paige asked. A minute after hearing the reply, she had turned away and was speaking softly into her headset, connecting to the shop. But the style was gone. Every single size.

Turning back to her client, Paige reached for the sandal. "I'll take care of it," she said in her most reassuring tone.

"I'm not wearing any other pair," the bride warned, her flawless face red with fury.

"Of course not," Paige said soothingly. Her calm, business-like manner was usually enough to settle an erupting bridezilla, a television creation that had spread alarmingly to ordinary women.

Paige took care not to mutter to herself or even shake her head as she headed out the open door of the church dressing room. At times like these, she began to dream of an easier line of work, like bar bouncer or snake handler.

Although both seemed an improvement, she had a job to do. And once alone in the vestibule, she dug into her satchel for what she needed.

Her secret weapon was the most powerful of glues, and she used it on everything from broken jewelry and headpieces to decorations. Although she had never tried it on shoes, she did not doubt its miraculous abilities.

However, since the bride might not share her confidence, Paige applied the remedy out of sight, then held the pieces together. After waiting several precious minutes, Paige slipped out of her footgear to test the results.

Although she wobbled in the ill-fitting high heels, the repair held. And just in time, she thought as she glanced at her watch.

Out of the corner of her eye, Paige saw a figure and hoped she hadn't been caught out. Putting her own shoe back on, she straightened and turned as if nothing were wrong. She'd rather be taken for a foot fetishist than admit to any problems with a wedding she was handling.

The genteel older woman who faced her did not appear dismayed but eyed her closely. Perhaps a little too closely.

Paige flashed a professional smile."May I be of help?"

The woman shook her head. "Thank you, dear, but I'll find an usher," she said, waving Paige away with an airy gesture. "You carry on."

Nodding, Paige hurried back toward the dressing room, but something made her glance over her shoulder. The well-dressed lady was staring after her, a knowing expression on her face.

Paige felt a pang of alarm. Would proof of the shoe debacle find its way online? But no. The guest held no phone. Nor did she look like the sort who would post an embarrassing moment for all to see. And yet, there was something odd about the encounter...

A whispered shriek from behind closed doors reminded Paige that she had more important things to worry about, and she forgot about the stranger. For now.

By the time the reception was nearly finished, Paige was setting her shoulders to keep from slumping over. But, despite a few glitches, the show had been a success, which could only do her business good. She savored that accomplishment even as she watched for any last-minute troubles.

"Ms. Porter?"

Paige turned to see the woman she had spoken to earlier in the vestibule, and her uneasiness returned. She braced herself for some kind of complaint about the seating, the food, the loudness of the music, etc., even as she summoned her professional smile.

But the woman did not look annoyed. At Paige's nod, she reached out to take her hand in a gentle clasp. "I'm Beatrice Maitland."

Her white hair was fashionably cut, her simple suit was tasteful, and she held herself in a manner that spoke of old money. Gesturing toward the linen-draped tables, festooned with white roses and crystal, and the gorgeous views of the bay beyond, she smiled.

"I'm very impressed."

"Thank you," Paige said, enjoying the rare praise. If anything went wrong, the wedding planner was always to blame, but few people noted a job well done.

The older woman studied her closely. "We need someone like you."

Paige's tiredness evaporated at the prospect of a new client, especially one like this woman: elegant, classy, moneyed...

"And perhaps you need us as well," Mrs. Maitland said.

Paige's smile faltered. Was her ambition showing?

"Well, we'll see," Mrs. Maitland said, with a graceful wave of her hand. "In the meantime, my granddaughter is engaged, and we could use your expertise. Nothing too elaborate. For several hundred guests, I would imagine."

Paige blinked at this unexpected opportunity, which might provide her the cachet she'd been lacking, an entrée into a more exclusive market.

"I'm sure you'll be able to manage quite nicely."

Paige nodded, trying not to look too eager. "Shall I give her a call?"

"Oh no," Mrs. Maitland said. "You had better come out to the house. You'll have to meet Siegfried, of course."

"The groom?" Paige asked.

Mrs. Maitland smiled. "Oh no, dear! Siegfried is my grandson. He's the one paying for it all."

Paige kept her face impassive as the woman handed her an elegant business card.

"Can you come tomorrow at five o'clock?"

Paige nodded, glancing down at the handwritten number on the back. And when she looked up, Mrs. Maitland was gone. Paige blinked but could not find her among the guests who were drifting off now that the bride and groom had been whisked away.

With a shake of her head, Paige realized the party was winding down and soon she could make her escape. As if on cue, her assistant Zoe appeared, hurrying toward her on ridiculously high heels.

Dark where Paige was fair, Zoe was the artistic heart of their enterprise. She had but one real goal: to marry well. Meanwhile, she enjoyed trying out her wedding day ideas on others. Her dream ceremony had blossomed accordingly, so that in order to pull off the envisioned event, she really *would* have to marry well.

Paige did not share her assistant's objective. Coming from a single-parent household, she was determined to rely on herself, not any man. And she'd been building her business with no other thought in mind, except perhaps the vague wish for a house of her own, which in the Bay Area required more cash than she had... yet.

"What were you doing with Bebe Maitland?" Zoe asked,

breathless from her race across the grass.

"Who?" Paige asked.

"Bebe—the matriarch of the whole Maitland family."

"Maitland family?" Paige echoed. As a displaced Midwesterner, the finer points of the city's social structure were sometimes lost on her.

"Hello? They're the Bay Area's resident clan of eccentrics, *rich* eccentrics," Zoe said, looking exasperated. But Paige was used to that look, which came when she didn't know the name of San Francisco's current Most Eligible Bachelor or what club was the hottest of the moment.

"How rich?" Paige asked, lifting her blond brows.

"Uh, billionaire rich!" Zoe said.

Paige felt the air leave her lungs at the prospect of arranging such a wedding. This could be the opportunity she'd been waiting for, she thought, turning over the card in her hand.

"The Maitland Company," she read aloud.

"Duh!" Zoe said. "The family founder was an inventor, plastics or explosives or something. Anyway, they've been raking in the money ever since."

The name did sound familiar. Paige stood staring at the lettering while Zoe expounded on how much Bebe gave to charity and how little anyone ever saw of the scions of the city, the "truly important," which in Zoe-speak probably meant "really eligible."

Paige tried not to get her hopes up too high, which was probably a good thing because Zoe suddenly fell silent. Since her assistant usually talked nonstop, that was never a good sign.

Paige glanced up to see that Zoe was wearing her thoughtful face, a sort of scrunched-up frown that would make anyone else look bad, except that Zoe was too gorgeous to ever look bad.

"What?" asked Paige, wondering if there was a catch. Was the granddaughter the sort of demanding, spoiled heiress who could make her job a living hell? Or was Bebe herself difficult? She had seemed a bit odd, though not in a bad way.

Zoe bit her lip. "Well, they are eccentric," she said.

"And what does that mean, exactly?" Paige asked, her eyes narrowing.

Zoe sighed and gave her an apologetic smile. "They're probably one of the weirdest families San Francisco's ever seen, and that's saying a lot."

The Maitland family was rich, all right. Paige stepped out of her subcompact onto the cobblestone drive and turned around, taking in the sprawling Tudor mansion poised high over the bay. The gate security had been state of the art, but now she felt as though she had stepped back in time—or into another world.

That sense of unreality continued when the door was opened by a very proper butler. Where were old-school servants like him found these days? Paige wondered as he invited her into the huge foyer. She supposed that money could buy anything, and the Maitlands obviously had plenty.

"Mrs. Maitland is expecting you, Ms. Porter," the man said in a staid British accent. Paige's innate cynicism kicked in, and she wondered if he really was from England.

He probably came from Livermore. Or maybe he was a displaced actor who had wandered up from L.A., she mused, only to see him lift his white brows as though well aware of her thoughts.

Chagrined, Paige stepped into an enormous entrance area where the walls rose to majestic heights designed to dazzle. Unfortunately, it was too dark for much dazzling. And the impressive expanse was lined with all sorts of antique weaponry, making it look like some weird hybrid of a chain restaurant and something maintained by the British Trust.

It was also cold and gloomy, Paige thought as she followed the butler down a long hallway. And it smelled funny. She sniffed discreetly. Was that incense?

Maybe drugs were at the root of the Maitlands' fabled eccentricities, and they were all sitting around smoking hash.

Paige tried to figure just how old Bebe was during Haight-Ashbury's heyday, but she couldn't picture the woman, who had to be in her seventies or eighties, doing anything so undignified.

Just when she thought she had made it through the incense, Paige's senses were assaulted anew, this time by the sound of unusual music accompanied by a screeching that jarred her eardrums. A particularly long wail made her haul up short. Were they torturing someone upstairs?

The hairs on the back of Paige's neck stood up as she wondered just what she had gotten herself into. Supposedly, the rich could do whatever they wanted, but now Paige wondered if that included kidnapping ordinary people, like wedding planners, and subjecting them to torment—or, at least, worse torment than her average client meted out.

Having noticed that she was no longer following him, the butler halted and turned. "That is Miss Woglinde," he intoned. Woglinde? Paige remained where she stood. "Mrs. Maitland's granddaughter," he explained.

At that moment the screeching reached a crescendo, lingered on a bloodcurdling note, then stopped as the music faded. Paige marveled at the butler's impassive countenance. Either he was deaf or he wore discreet earplugs.

As though reading her thoughts again, the man drew himself up, his elegant tailcoat making him look even more impressive. "She is practicing her Verdi," he said. "She fancies herself an opera singer."

The man's proper British pronunciation and sober countenance held no hint of sarcasm, a feat that Paige could only admire. Even when sung by professionals, opera sounded like caterwauling to her, but this was positively painful.

When the singing resumed, she nearly put her hands over her ears. Only the thought of what this wedding could do for her business made Paige step forward once more, her teeth firmly gritted.

Thankfully, the sound faded as they moved farther into the house, a maze that Paige would never have mastered on her own. When the butler stopped before the carved doors of what he called the parlor, Paige decided that the place could be right out of the who-done-it board game she had loved as a kid. There were no dead bodies, of course, though there were plenty of weapons in the foyer.

And there might be some secret passages, Paige realized, intrigued in spite of herself. The Maitland home was old-school, not one of the new McMansions with their cold beige and white spaces. The house had character, even though the character needed a face-lift, Paige thought, as the butler announced her arrival.

"Ah, Ms. Porter. How lovely to see you again."

The sight of the distinguished-looking Mrs. Maitland made Paige dismiss her earlier notions. The older woman wore a stunning suit and a cordial expression. She did not look like the owner of a drug den or torture chamber.

With an answering smile, Paige stepped forward. "Thank you for inviting me to your home. It's beautiful."

"It was built by my husband's father in the early part of the last century when property was plentiful and cheap. Thankfully, the family has managed to hang on to it," Mrs. Maitland said.

The family probably could do more than that, including building something twice as big, Paige thought. But they would be hard-pressed to find a better location. And there was an Old World charm to the place even though it begged for a bit of improving, such as a good cleaning—and a ban on armaments as decor.

Mrs. Maitland turned toward the butler. "Thank you, Godfrey. Would you bring us some refreshments, please?"

The butler's name was Godfrey? Like the movie *My Man Godfrey*? About a butler? Now Paige was sure he wasn't for real as she darted him a startled glance.

"What would you like, Ms. Porter? Some lemonade? Iced tea? Perhaps a fruit drink or some soda?" Mrs. Maitland asked.

Paige opted for a diet cola, while Mrs. Maitland requested

an iced tea. "Oh, and Godfrey, do you know where Siegfried might be found?"

"I believe he is on the terrace, Mrs. Maitland," the man said, his face impassive. Although he looked the part of a family retainer of long standing, Paige eyed him curiously.

"Thank you. We shall go out, then."

The butler nodded, and Paige wondered about servants in general. How could you hang around the house in sweats while other people were looking on? Obviously, you couldn't run around naked or in your underwear. It was kind of creepy, she decided, but maybe only if you had a butler. Named Godfrey.

"Shall we go out on the terrace?" Mrs. Maitland asked, gesturing with a delicate hand.

"I'd love to," Paige said, eager to clear her head. The Maitland household was eccentric all right, but the rich were different, she reminded herself. And at least outside they would be well out of earshot of the opera singer—and inhaling distance of the incense.

"Please call me Bebe," the older woman said.

"Paige."

"Well, Paige, the fog often keeps us cool, but today should be pleasantly warm," Bebe said, opening the French doors.

Nodding, Paige stepped out and nearly swallowed her tongue. The view was breathtaking. Beyond the stone terrace and elaborate gardens, the earth fell away, and the bay met the sky.

Tall sycamores draped in ferns shaded old iron benches, and paths meandered through patches of sunshine and colorful blooms, with a low stone wall as backdrop. In all her years of wedding planning, Paige had never seen a more perfect spot for staging nuptials.

Although there was no denying her initial impression, closer scrutiny revealed that, like the building itself, the garden was looking a little shabby around the edges. Everything was a bit overgrown, as though the Maitlands had abandoned the upkeep.

It would all need some work before the event, but the sense

of encroaching wilderness appealed to Paige. Up here the crowded, hectic city was far away, and the only sounds were those of the birds.

Paige took in a deep breath of fresh air, only to start as the peaceful afternoon was broken by a clacking noise, like that of a rickety train heading in her direction. As she watched wide-eyed, the leaves of a tall, flowering bush were abruptly thrust out of the way.

Paige froze. Weren't there reports of mountain lions attacking hikers up in these hills? And who knew what kind of menageries these uber-wealthy people kept around? From the condition of the grounds, any pens to hold such animals had deteriorated to the point of uselessness, unleashing lions, tigers, and bears upon unsuspecting wedding planners.

Oh my.

CHAPTER TWO

Paige's good sense asserted itself as she realized no wild beast could make such a metallic din. Just one animal could be responsible: man.

But her relief was short-lived as that man burst through the foliage like he had been shot from a rocket. For a moment, Paige thought the guy *had* erupted from a circus canon, for he seemed to be suspended in air. And all she could do was stare in horror as he hurtled straight toward her.

Everything seemed to move in slow motion, yet Paige barely had time to register the look of surprise on her attacker's face. Perhaps he had planned to rob Mrs. Maitland, only to be faced with a far younger and poorer target.

Whatever his intent, at the sight of her he suddenly twisted his body, slamming against her side. She was knocked to the ground anyway, though without the full force of his weight. But he was heavy enough as it was, what with more than six feet of him lying half over her.

The wind had been knocked from her, so Paige struggled to take a breath, pulling into her lungs the smell of warm male. Somehow the weight didn't feel so bad after all, she thought, only to catch herself. Had she inhaled too much incense? Or had the fall scrambled her brains?

Rather than lying there like some dazed lover, Paige knew she ought to be doing something to stop this guy. After all, he hadn't fallen out of the sky, even if it had looked that way. He must have some kind of agenda, most likely assault and robbery upon the wealthy Maitlands.

But Paige didn't feel like moving. The stone was cool against her back, and there was something strangely comforting about the man's body, emanating heat and strength and a delicious low groan. Or maybe it had just been too long since she'd had sex.

"Siegfried! Paige, are you all right?"

At the sound of Mrs. Maitland's voice, the body atop hers stirred and rolled away, and Paige couldn't stifle a sigh of disappointment. Maybe she had a concussion.

As she lay there blinking into the sunlight, two faces appeared overhead, blocking out the clouds. One, older and female, was that of a concerned Bebe. The other, younger and male, was that of the man who struck her.

But somehow he looked concerned, too. Or, at least, very serious. What kind of a criminal was he?

"Can you hear me?" he asked.

"Oh, Siegfried, what have you done now? Try to help her up. Godfrey!" Bebe called.

"We shouldn't move her. She might be injured," the man said.

He was handsome, Paige realized, his high cheekbones and even features a bit obscured by shaggy dark hair—nice, shaggy, dark hair. In fact, he had that "good guy" look to him, which obviously wasn't true, since he was a burglar or something. Paige's brows furrowed.

"Well, I think it is obvious that she's injured," Bebe said.

As Paige blinked up at him, Good-looking Guy reached for her, and she felt his hands run lightly up her arms and legs. Delightfully warm again, she enjoyed his capable yet gentle touch until she realized she probably ought to be alarmed at such treatment.

Maybe this was all part of the Maitlands' infamous eccentricity and soon she'd be upstairs screeching in torment, like the so-called opera singer. But Paige suspected this kind of torment resulted in screaming of an entirely different sort.

"What are you doing?" Bebe asked.

"Checking for broken bones," the good-looking bad guy said. His voice was nice, not too deep, not too high, not oily or raspy, just good. In fact, everything was good about him, except his badness, of course.

Paige smiled.

"It's not her bones. It's her head, Siegfried. I fear she's dazed," Bebe said, her voice rising.

"Yes, madam?" A British accent announced that the butler had arrived.

"Oh, Godfrey, there you are!" Bebe said, obviously flustered. "Please call 911. Ms. Porter has been injured."

"For God's sake, don't call a doctor." A new voice carried to Paige's ears, a female one laced with cigarette huskiness, and indeed, Paige could smell smoke. Normal smoke. And no incense.

"How many times have I warned you about lawsuits? If you call 911, you can kiss another couple million goodbye."

"But, Mia, dear. Siegfried knocked her down."

"That's why you shouldn't invite anyone to the house, Bebe. He's hopeless, a complete social misfit."

Paige tried to block out all the voices and concentrate on Good-looking Guy, who was attempting to get her attention.

"How many fingers am I holding up?" he asked her, his low tone sliding deliciously along her senses.

"Two," she whispered.

"Wrong answer! You should have said three if you wanted the millions," the cigarette smoker said.

"Mia, really! Paige is here to help us," Bebe scolded.

Good-looking Guy's luscious lips curved slightly, just enough to make Paige want to melt into the patio, which she took as a sign that she wasn't herself. She never melted, especially where a guy was concerned, even a good-looking bad one.

Paige blinked, suddenly confused as to why her assailant was hovering over her, especially since no one seemed to mind. She sat up.

"Do you think that's wise, dear? You might have a concussion," Bebe murmured.

"Don't give her any ideas!"

Turning her head, Paige found the speaker, a slender platinum blonde who was smoking a cigarette. She had a sort of brittle beauty and looked like a spoiled heiress. And considering her rudeness, Paige couldn't summon even a business smile.

"Look. She's just fine," the girl said, with a smirk.

"Well, she does seem to be better now," Bebe said. "Godfrey, don't call 911. But bring a cold compress for Ms. Porter."

"I don't know how that is going to help," the Good-looking Guy said.

"Well, she hit her head, didn't she?"

To Paige's delight, Good-looking Guy put a hand to her hair and felt gently around the back of her head.

"There is no lump," he said.

"There goes your case," the heiress said.

"Of course, a cold compress won't help if there is swelling in the brain," Good-looking Guy said. Paige might have been alarmed if she hadn't been so fascinated with his mouth. Besides, she hadn't even hit her head. "You might want to get a CT scan."

"Perhaps I should have Arthur take her to the hospital," Bebe said.

"It's your money," the heiress said with disdain before flicking a cigarette butt into the bushes.

"Mia, dear, I wish you wouldn't do that," Bebe said. "That's why Alphonse quit. Our gardener," she added, smiling at Paige.

"What is going on here?"

At the sound of a deep bellow, Paige turned. Through the French doors stepped a very large man dressed in linen pants and a velvet jacket, with a silk scarf draped around his neck.

"Woglinde cannot concentrate with such a commotion," he said, in what sounded like a really bad Italian accent.

Paige blinked. Maybe she *had* hit her head.

"This girl's going to take the family for millions with some bogus accident claim," the heiress said, pointing at Paige.

"It isn't a claim. She did have an accident," Bebe protested.

Having gathered at least some of her wits, Paige decided she had had enough of the heiress's bad-mouthing. "I am not making any claim or taking any money," she said.

Unless it's for an indecently extravagant wedding, she added silently. She rose to her feet, with the help of Good-looking Guy, and turned toward the heiress, who shrugged.

"Paige, dear, this is my great-niece Mia," Bebe said. "She's staying here until she sorts things out with her family."

"There's nothing to sort out," Mia said. "They're assholes."

"Now, my dear," Bebe said. "That's no way to talk about the Andersons."

Mia... Anderson? Paige blinked. Mia Anderson *was* a spoiled heiress and a notorious party girl whose antics filled the gossip columns. Surely, she wasn't the one who was getting married? Paige wobbled on her feet at that vision of the Client From Hell.

Thankfully, Good-looking Guy was there to help, and he maneuvered her toward one of the antique wicker chairs scattered about the enormous patio. Paige leaned back, glad to be seated, but bemoaning the loss of those big hands as they left her.

"Really, Mia," Bebe began, only to stop as the butler appeared with a silver platter that he presented to her, his face impassive.

"What is this, Godfrey?" Bebe asked, looking dubiously at the offering.

"It is a sack of frozen peas, madam," he said.

"Frozen peas? Why would I want frozen peas?" Bebe asked.

"There are no more cold compresses, madam, and Mrs. Bates suggested the frozen vegetables might make a suitable replacement."

"Well, they don't. Please take them away," Bebe said with a shudder. "Unless..." She turned a questioning look upon Paige.

"No. I'm fine, really. I just had the breath knocked out of me," Paige said. Good-looking Guy was still hovering, and she wondered if mouth-to-mouth was part of his revival skills. A girl could hope, couldn't she?

"But you are hurt, you poor child," the pseudo Italian said, eyeing her with a little too much interest.

"Paige, this is Lorenzo, Woglinde's opera instructor."

"And a celebrated performer in my own right," the man said, swooping into a bow.

"Paige is here to plan the wedding," Bebe said.

"Ah. I am enchanted to meet you, my child," he said, stepping toward her. Paige had the feeling he was going to try to kiss her hand or something equally bizarre, but he was stopped by a warning from Bebe.

"Oh dear, Lorenzo. Watch where you are going," she said, looking pointedly at something blocking the man's path.

For one so large, Lorenzo was nimble. He swooped down to pick up the object with a distasteful frown."I suppose this is the culprit, the cause of this poor, unfortunate young woman's calamity."

His effusive description made Paige look curiously at what he held, and she blinked at what appeared to be a skateboard.

"Do not tell me you were attempting to ride this thing?" Lorenzo demanded. He turned toward Good-looking Guy, and Paige followed his gaze. Who ever heard of a skateboarding burglar? But if he was an intruder, why did everyone seem to know him?

"Paige, this is my grandson Siegfried," Bebe said, effectively resolving the mystery. "I'm sure he didn't mean to knock you down."

"Or wreck the magnificent terrace!" Lorenzo said, shaking his head. Under his breath, he was murmuring snippets of Italian. Or was it something about "a lunatic"?

Paige was relieved to know that Good-looking Guy wasn't an assailant until she realized that no one over the age of eighteen ought to be riding a skateboard, especially along the antique wrought-iron railings of a multimillion-dollar estate, where innocent visitors were standing.

But at least no one was staring at her any longer; they were all looking at the board, which was offensive in itself. It was worn, dirty, and covered with writing, including the large black scrawl of a four-letter word that Paige didn't think ought to be used in front of Bebe.

Swallowing a sigh, Paige glanced from the board to Siegfried and realized that Zoe was right again. Didn't she swear that any handsome man in the Bay Area had to be married, gay, or unacceptable? Lunacy would definitely fall into that last category.

"Where did you get this?" Lorenzo asked, his distaste evident as he released the board. But Siegfried snatched it up. He did seem to be good with those hands.

"I saw someone riding it in an abandoned parking lot," he explained.

Lorenzo shuddered. Pulling a massive handkerchief from the pocket of what looked like an old-school smoking jacket, he carefully wiped his fingers.

"So I had Arthur stop," Siegfried said. Dropping the board to the pavement, he paid no more heed to his former victim. Paige was tempted to moan just to regain his attention until she remembered that he might be a lunatic.

"You stopped in some abandoned parking lot and accosted a skateboarder?" Mia asked, snorting.

"At first he thought I was going to confiscate his board or gank it, as he put it, but eventually we came to an agreement."

"How much?" Mia asked.

"I gave him a hundred dollars for it."

Mia shook her head. "I thought he wasn't allowed to carry money," she said, turning to Bebe.

"I had to get it from Arthur," Siegfried said as he balanced on the board in ratty sneakers.

This guy was wealthy? Paige wondered before answering her own question. Oh, yeah, and he was also a lunatic.

"He's lucky the kid didn't knife him," Mia said, with a dismissive glance.

Obviously bored now that a lawsuit was no longer imminent, the heiress turned and disappeared through the French doors. The butler had gone, too, taking the frozen peas with him, but he had left the tray of refreshments.

"There seems to be some degree of skill involved," Siegfried muttered as he pushed across the flagstones, his tall form slouching, his shirttail hanging over a pair of worn jeans. He was definitely not attractively dressed, and Paige wondered why she'd been so enamored.

She blamed the fall.

Still, she watched him for a long moment as he stood poised over the board, lean muscle sometimes evident under his baggy clothes. Absorbed in his task, he seemed to be able to ignore everyone else, as well as the damage he might be doing to the terrace. But why wouldn't he? He was a lunatic.

"Please, enjoy your drink," Bebe said, pressing the diet cola on Paige. But instead of taking a seat next to her, the Maitland matriarch remained standing, looking over the scene of Siegfried's destruction with a pensive expression.

"I'm afraid you'll have to excuse me," she said. "After all the excitement, I think I'll have a lie-down."

Paige glanced at her in surprise. Maybe the older woman wasn't as strong as she looked. Or maybe being knocked to the ground by her grandson had put Paige out of the running for the job.

"I can come back another time," Paige hastened to offer. Although the thought of returning to this madhouse made her shudder, she would do it for a chance at the business.

"Oh no! There's no need for that," Bebe said. "You can work things out with Siegfried."

Paige gaped at the older woman. "But, uh, what about the bride?"

"Oh, I'll see if I can find Flosshilde," Bebe said. She waved her hand in the air as if the presence of at least one member of the engaged couple was unimportant.

"She's probably posing again."

At the sound of Lorenzo's voice, Paige's head whipped around. She'd forgotten the presence of the singing instructor who had moved closer while her attention was elsewhere.

"Flosshilde spends much of her time modeling for her fiancé," Bebe explained. "He is an artist, you see."

Paige kept her face composed even as she wondered just

how many, uh, eccentrics lived here. If the groom-to-be was as much an artist as Woglinde was an opera singer, he probably spent his time making crayon drawings. In fact, Paige was surprised he wasn't here with chalk, defacing the terrace alongside Siegfried.

"I shall see if I can find her for you," Lorenzo offered. Although he bent low again as if to make some Old World gesture, Paige kept her hands firmly out of his reach.

She could hardly protest when the two of them went inside the house, but their pledges to search for the bride did not sound promising. Meanwhile, Paige was alone with the lunatic, who was skateboarding along a quaint stone wall in complete disregard of its beauty, as well as her presence.

How was she to talk wedding plans with him? Paige tried to remember what little her assistant had told her about the Maitland heir. She knew that he was a boy genius, a brilliant inventor, reclusive, and, well, eccentric.

But it appeared that Zoe had failed to mention one more thing, which was uppermost in Paige's mind as she contemplated doing business with the guy.

Siegfried Maitland was dangerous.

CHAPTER THREE

Paige told herself that Siegfried Maitland was a menace because of his outlandish behavior, but the danger he posed involved more than his skateboarding skills. She couldn't remember the last time she had been distracted from her work, let alone by a guy.

Sipping her soda, Paige eyed him critically. Now that he was wobbling along the wall, he didn't seem that threatening—or even good-looking. Hunched over the board, hair hanging in his face, he resembled nothing so much as a gangly high school kid who was ignoring her. And Paige didn't like playing the part of the adult who must wrangle his attention.

In fact, she felt a cowardly urge to flee the whole Maitland compound and all of its inhabitants, especially this one. Only the prospect of a sweet job and what it could mean to her business kept her in place.

High-end weddings commanded high-end prices, and with a few of them, Paige might be able to buy her own place. Even if it was only a tiny condo, she could have somewhere to call her own for the first time in her life. Secure. Permanent. Home.

Paige was jolted from her daydream by the sight of Siegfried taking a dive into an overgrown hydrangea. She looked around, but there was no one else outside, so she stood up slowly, a bit uncertain after her own fall.

When everything seemed to be in working order, she walked to the old wall, where she found him lying on his back in the grass, staring up at the sky as though he had never seen it before.

Paige leaned over him. "Are you okay?"

He blinked as though he had never seen her before, either, and Paige wondered whether she should call for help. But then those eyes focused on her, and she couldn't even force out a squeak. They were as warm and delicious as hot chocolate and just as inviting.

They kept staring at her, not in a lunatic way, but with such guileless intensity that Paige felt like they could see right inside her. The idea was ridiculous, of course, and yet she stared back, filled with an absurd yearning, until her good sense made her glance away.

But Siegfried continued to lie there, prostrate in the grass. Was this typical genius behavior? Or had the guy taken too many falls off his board? Since he made no move to rise, Paige began to wonder if he was hurt.

"Can you get up?" she asked, extending a hand uncertainly.

"Oh, yeah. Thanks," he said, as though he had forgotten his prone position or his ability to stand upright. His big hand clasped hers, and Paige felt a surge of heat as he swung to his feet with an easy grace.

"There seems to be a problem with my rotational inertia," he said, leaning down to retrieve the board.

"What?" Paige whispered. Her voice had lost its professional tone, probably because she was uncomfortable standing so close to such an erratic character. It certainly wasn't because she caught a whiff of the warm male that had been lying on top of her not that long ago.

"The dynamics," he said, holding up the skateboard.

Not that again. Paige drew in a head-clearing breath. "Aren't you a little old for this sort of thing?"

He shrugged. Now that he had turned his attention elsewhere, Paige felt a sense of loss, as though she were competing with a slab of wood with wheels. She frowned.

"I thought boys went through the skateboarding stage before puberty, so they could show off on the school playground."

"I didn't go to school," Siegfried said. "My mother didn't believe in the modern educational paradigm."

Paige blinked. No wonder the guy was eccentric. She'd known kids who were homeschooled early on, but later? "What about high school? Proms and football games?"

Siegfried shook his head.

Paige swallowed hard. Of course, the rich were different. "Prep school?"

"No time. I was in college instead," Siegfried said, rubbing at the edge of a particularly nasty gouge in the wood.

Paige was watching his fingers, so it took her a moment to realize that he really was a boy genius, the kind who got his degree at age twelve or something. She glanced up at his unlined face and wondered how old he was.

He looked like he was in his mid-twenties, but she supposed he could be just a teenager. The thought appalled her for some reason, probably because she wasn't used to working with someone who couldn't legally drink.

"Ah, there she is!"

Paige flushed at the sound of another voice, though there was certainly no crime in studying her client, or at least the guy footing the bill. But somehow she was way too close to him, so she stepped back and looked toward the house.

She could see Lorenzo standing near the French doors with a slender young woman Paige could only hope was the bride-to-be. He waved her over, and Paige welcomed the return to business.

Although she considered herself personable, there was such a thing as getting too personal in her line of work. It was best to keep a certain distance from everyone involved, or you could find yourself, as Zoe sometimes did, getting caught up in the dramas.

Setting her shoulders, Paige approached the two with a smile on her face, relieved to meet the client at last. She hadn't even reached them before Lorenzo swept forward into an expansive gesture.

"My dear Paige, this is Woglinde," he said, as though presenting a member of royalty—or a famous diva. His companion certainly looked the part.

She was dressed as oddly as Lorenzo, in a floaty, scarf-like creation that made her look much older than Siegfried. Her dark hair was coiled tightly at the back of her head, and she flashed so much jewelry that Paige was nearly blinded.

"Ms. Paige?" she said, with a lift of her dark brows.

Was that an accent, or was the young woman just taking on Lorenzo's? "Ms. Porter. But please call me Paige."

"Paige," she echoed. "I am Woglinde, and I have some ideas for Flosshilde's ceremony."

"Excuse me?" Hadn't Lorenzo gone in search of the bride-to-be? Paige was beginning to wonder if she had blacked out and was dreaming this whole scenario. But there's no way she could have come up with such names.

"You are the wedding planner, aren't you?" Woglinde asked in a haughty tone.

"Yes. I'm sorry," Paige said, recovering herself. "I thought you were the bride-to-be."

Lorenzo laughed, and the diva frowned. "Not I. I have my career to think about, and it will always come before any man."

Perhaps it wasn't an accent, just perfect diction that made the woman sound odd. Paige opened her mouth to ask politely about the career until she realized this must be the opera wannabe. Fearing a demonstration, Paige promptly snapped her teeth together.

"But I do have some suggestions," Woglinde said.

While Paige forced a smile, she groaned inwardly. Too much input from those not directly involved made for a difficult assignment, awkward juggling, and hurt feelings that could lead to the aforementioned drama. But she dutifully took a seat, as did Lorenzo and Woglinde.

The diva leaned forward, with an intensity far more unsettling than Siegfried's. And for some reason, her brown eyes weren't as arresting, either, as she fixed them on Paige. Once assured of her audience's attention, she paused, as if preparing to make an earth-shattering announcement, and Paige braced herself.

"I would like to restage La Boheme, or at least a portion of it, with all the guests dressed in appropriate costume, of course."

Paige blinked. "An opera-themed wedding? That's... unique," she said, trying not to look horrified. She could only gape in astonishment as Woglinde laid out her plan, including the plot and the staging. In addition to the outlandish clothing that would be required, Woglinde fancied herself in the leading woman's role, which included a death scene.

"I'm sorry, but I just don't think the subject lends itself to a wedding celebration," Paige said. She always tried her best to give the clients what they wanted, but if that wasn't possible, it was her job to convince them that they wanted something else.

And Paige was all for the latter. She was hoping to improve her business, not sabotage it, and she'd have to step down if the Maitlands wanted such a production. But she wasn't at all sure they did, especially since she had yet to talk to the engaged couple.

"What does your sister think?" Paige asked.

Woglinde waved a hand in dismissal. "She's not equal to the part."

"I mean, what sort of wedding does she want? Have you discussed the opera idea with her?" Paige asked.

"Perhaps Flosshilde would prefer Das Rheingold," Lorenzo said.

"Oh, that's so expected," Woglinde said, with another airy wave of her hand. When Paige eyed her blankly, she sighed. "You do realize that we are the Rhinemaidens."

"I beg your pardon?"

"We were named after the Rhinemaidens in Das Rheingold. It was Father's favorite opera."

Paige wondered whether the man was still alive or if his progeny had killed him once they hit junior high. Oh, but they hadn't attended school, had they? Reminded suddenly of Siegfried, Paige glanced around the grounds and didn't see him.

"And your brother?" she asked, with a wary eye on the bushes.

"Obviously, Siegfried takes his name from the piece, too,"

Woglinde said.

"But he is not one of the Rhinemaidens," Lorenzo pointed out.

"Of course not," Woglinde said, frowning. "But Das Rheingold is too long, Lorenzo. And you can't just chop it up into bits for the ceremony."

"I suppose not." Lorenzo nodded seriously.

Paige's head was spinning. She took a deep breath. "Look, Woglinde... Do you mind if I call you Linde?"

The diva appeared to be taken aback. "I suppose not."

"Thank you. Linde, I think you have some interesting views, but I don't really want to pursue anything until I talk to the bride-to-be," Paige said.

She launched into standard wedding-speak. "After all, she is the one getting married, and a woman's wedding is a once-in-a-lifetime experience. Usually, my clients feel very strongly about what they want for their perfect day."

Linde frowned, as though unused to being crossed, or at least, held at bay.

"I'm afraid that Flosshilde is modeling," Lorenzo said. "And her fiancé does not like to be interrupted when he is creating."

Great. "Perhaps I could make an appointment," Paige suggested.

"Good luck," Linde said, rising from her chair. "Come, Lorenzo. Let us resume our exercises."

Lorenzo bowed graciously. "Good-bye, my dear."

Paige saw her contacts disappearing yet again and her hopes for her business going with them. She shot to her feet.

"Wait! Isn't there anyone I can talk to about scheduling a meeting with the couple? Surely, Mrs. Maitland has a secretary or an assistant."

"No. I'm afraid not," Lorenzo said. He motioned Paige closer, as if he could not speak openly, although no one except Woglinde was within hearing distance.

"She has been through five in the last few years," he said in a low voice. "They've all been very unreliable, so she has given up on hiring anyone."

Paige frowned. Although she could guess why an employee might not stick around this wacky household, she needed to be able to reach someone. And she couldn't disturb her hostess.

"What about the butler?"

"Godfrey?" Linde asked, with an expression of distaste. "You may try, of course, but he will say it's not in his job description."

"Which seems to be quite brief," Lorenzo added.

Paige was still trying to think of someone else when they closed the French doors behind them, leaving her on the terrace. With a sigh, she turned around to face a world gone very quiet. Peaceful. Serene.

There was only the sound of the birds and the wind rustling through the trees, and for a long moment, Paige enjoyed the sensation of being alone in this little corner of paradise.

Then she remembered Siegfried.

CHAPTER FOUR

Where had the boy genius gone? Paige glanced around the grounds but didn't see him, and she knew he hadn't passed her. Although there were probably lots of other entrances to the house, she still would have noticed him, right?

What if he had crashed again? She hadn't heard anything, but she had been busy with Linde and Lorenzo.

With a twinge of panic, Paige set out among the paths, searching for benches or rails that might tempt a boarder. She made a slow circuit, finding nothing, only to end up at the low stone wall where she had last seen him. The one that overlooked the cliffs.

Bracing herself, Paige looked for his mangled body below, but there was no sign of him. Clumps of tall grass obscured some of the beach, so she called his name, softly at first, then louder. Just in case.

She listened for any groans emanating from the bushes, but the drone of insects and the lap of the waves were all that answered her. Finally, Paige leaned her arms on the old stone, took a deep breath of ocean-scented air, and gazed out over the water to enjoy a view unequaled.

"I see you've recovered."

That cigarette-roughened voice could only belong to one person, and Paige turned to see Mia Anderson standing on the edge of the terrace, giving her the eye.

"Yes," Paige said, refusing to be intimidated by someone whose bad-girl antics were fueled by too much time and money. "I was just wondering about Siegfried. He seems to have disappeared."

Mia appeared unconcerned. She shrugged one slender shoulder and pulled on her cigarette. In person she looked way too thin, but weren't all those tabloid girls anorexic?

"I wouldn't worry about him," the heiress said. "He's a big

boy."

Really? Paige wondered again just how big... er, old he was. And no matter what his age, he didn't seem to be the kind of guy who took good care of himself. She peered over the wall again. "I hope he didn't fall off."

"If he did, we'll all be that much richer. Or his sisters will be, anyway," Mia said, with a show of indifference.

"The Rhinemaidens," Paige said.

"Yes, Woglinde, Wellgunde, and Flosshilde," Mia said. Then she grimaced. "Don't tell me you're an opera fan."

"Not really," Paige admitted.

"Woglinde's the only one around," Mia said. "Flosshilde spends most of her time shut up with her fiancé, rolling around among the drop cloths or whatever. Wellgunde is at school back East."

"I see," Paige said, silently thanking her mother for her name.

"You can find out for yourself at dinner."

"What?" Paige asked, flustered by the notion that the heiress was asking her to stay.

"Hey, it's not my idea. It's Bebe's," Mia said, making her feelings clear.

Paige's first instinct was to refuse such a dubious invitation and return to her own little efficiency apartment, simple, unpretentious and decidedly normal. But what about her dream job? How was she to get it if she hadn't even met the client?

"Thanks, I'd be happy to join you," Paige said. She took a step forward only to stop when a certain anxiety returned to nag at her. "But what about Siegfried?"

Mia shrugged, obviously uncaring. "He probably lost interest in his new toy."

His skateboard, Paige told herself before she could think anything else. *She's talking about his skateboard.*

"Sometimes he doesn't eat for days," the heiress added, blowing smoke.

Paige was horrified at the casual observation, which would

explain why Siegfried looked gangly. The guy needed feeding, though he hadn't felt too skinny when lying on top of her, Paige remembered. However, she had been knocked out of breath—and maybe out of her head—at the time.

"Hey, you can go look for him if you want," Mia suggested.

The change in her tone, from snarky to faux friendly, made Paige wary. "I already have."

Mia rolled her eyes at Paige's efforts, then fixed her with an insolent stare. "He's probably in his underground laboratory."

"What?" Now Paige knew Mia was messing with her.

But the heiress didn't laugh. "His lab," she said with a smirk. "It's in the catacombs under the house. The cliff is riddled with them." She flicked her butt onto the terrace.

Paige wanted to strangle the heiress for littering the grounds—and taunting a guest. "Maybe I will look for him," she said, taking up the challenge.

"Suit yourself," Mia said with a shrug. "There's a path on the other side of the wall, by the gate."

Before Paige could ask for particulars, the girl turned back to the house and went inside, leaving her with nothing to do except make good on her promise. Heaving a sigh, Paige walked along the wall until she found the old wrought-iron gate. Getting it to move was a bit tricky, however, and she was forced to throw her weight against it repeatedly.

When it finally swung open, she almost went sprawling down the steep hill. Digging in her heels, Paige watched a stray pebble she had dislodged bounce all the way to the narrow stretch of beach below, and she swallowed hard.

She was already regretting her impulsive decision. How had she let herself be goaded into this? She was usually sensible—too sensible, according to Zoe. But she hadn't felt like herself since falling.

Now, she just wanted to avoid an even worse tumble, for it soon became apparent that the word "path" was a misnomer. The slabs of stone set into the side of the hill petered out, disappearing into clumps of grass, and Paige was forced to find her own footholds.

Eventually, she was reduced to scrambling down the side of the cliff like a mountain goat, hoping that she wouldn't break her neck in the process.

By the time she reached the sand, Paige was tired, sweaty, and dirty from a couple of slips. Her dress-to-impress suit was the worse for wear, and she had nearly lost one of the shoes that Zoe had insisted she borrow.

Paige was in no mood for any of the Maitland weirdness. In fact, she was prepared to tell the head weirdo, Siegfried himself, just what he could do with his skateboard. Surely, no wedding was worth this kind of suffering.

Unfortunately, Siegfried was not at the bottom of the cliff. After bending over to massage the cramp in her leg and catch her breath, Paige realized the shoreline was uninhabited except by sea birds.

Where were the caves that supposedly riddled the cliffs? Had Mia Anderson sent her down here as a joke?

If so, Paige would find out from Zoe just where to peddle her personal story about the heiress. She could just see the headline now: *Mia Sends Wedding Planner to Her Death.* Okay, so maybe she couldn't write the story if that were true. Instead, she'd have to go with *Mia Leaves Wedding Planner to Die.*

Paige gritted her teeth. The way she felt right now the headline was more likely to read *Wedding Planner Attacks Heiress.* Hopefully, Paige could manage to yank out some of the girl's dyed hair when she did so.

A glance at the so-called path down which she had come made Paige flinch. She couldn't imagine making her way back up, especially in these heels.

She might take them off and try to cling to the dirt with her toes, pulling herself up by some of the shocks of long grass. But if they didn't hold, she could crash over some rocks, which was not an appealing prospect. Even if she lived, she couldn't very well go about her job in a body cast.

"Hello?" Paige called, despite her isolation. Although not

far from one of the greatest cities in the world, she might as well have been on the moon. And the gorgeous view she had admired from the grounds now seemed a vaguely threatening landscape.

Suddenly, Paige wondered if the tide was in or whether she'd have to crawl back up just to escape it. *Okay, Paige, don't panic,* she told herself. She had been in predicaments before, although they usually involved wayward florists and inadequate seating.

She could always call Bebe, Paige thought, and she reached for her cell phone, only to remember that it was tucked into the purse she had left on the terrace. After cursing her carelessness, she decided there was little Bebe could do anyway except send Godfrey rappelling down after her. Or Siegfried.

The image of the Maitland heir as a latter-day Tarzan, swinging Paige to safety, was momentarily arresting. But he was more likely to pull a George of the Jungle and slam her into a cliff, if he came to her rescue at all, which was doubtful.

However, thoughts of the guy made Paige call out his name again, even though he couldn't be anywhere within hearing distance... unless he was in the supposed catacombs. If the heiress hadn't punked her, maybe Siegfried was here, hidden from view, and all she had to do was look.

But as soon as she stepped away from the grassy slope, Paige sank. Literally. Before she realized what was happening, she was stuck, her heels sucked so deep that she finally had to slip out of the shoes.

Bending over, she yanked Zoe's expensive footwear out of the sand and frowned at the sight. They were definitely looking a little worse for wear.

Dangling them in one hand, Paige began walking along the shore, studying the face of the cliff for clues. She felt ridiculous, like some character out of a spy movie, but as she rounded an outcropping, something caught her eye. It was tucked under an overhang, nothing but a shadowy crevice at first sight, but when Paige moved closer, she stood gaping in astonishment.

On this deserted bit of sand, in the middle of a rocky cliff, was an elaborately carved Tudor-style door. Paige turned around, half expecting to see Mia smirking behind her, along with a crew filming her practical joke. But only boats bobbed in the distance, and eventually the beach ran out.

It took Paige a good minute to realize she had met with success and wouldn't have to crawl back up to the house. Then she reached toward the worn wood, only to discover there was no knob or pull or lever of any kind.

Was the door just decoration? Some long-forgotten worker's entrance? A remnant of prohibition bootlegging? No, it's a secret lab, Paige reminded herself.

So what was she to do, make like Nancy Drew and tap the surfaces for hidden latches? *Speak Friend and Enter*, she thought, recalling a line from one of her favorite books.

But she didn't suppose saying "friend" would help. And since Siegfried was a boy genius with a bankroll, entry could require anything from reciting Klingon to an eyeball scan.

Or she could just go old-school. With a sigh, Paige shifted the shoes to her other hand, lifted a fist, and knocked. The rap sounded loud in the stillness, startling some gulls overhead. Of course, she didn't really expect anyone to answer, but she held her breath, just in case.

Nothing happened.

Although Paige prided herself for her cool under pressure, this whole experience was a little more taxing than the average wedding. Suddenly, her frayed nerves snapped and she began banging on the door as hard as she could with one of the shoes.

Only when the heel broke off did she stop, horrified. Her very own shoe crisis, and she had no glue. Zoe was going to kill her—if she didn't die here first.

Just as that ominous thought formed, the door swung inward and Paige sprang back. Although relieved to see some sign of life, she was wary. After all, this was not a typical entranceway, and hadn't Mia mentioned catacombs? Paige half expected to see a hunchback lurch out of a dark cavern or a vampire fly from its coffin.

However, gloom did not greet her, only a harsh white light so bright it made her blink. And the man who stood just inside was not Igor or the Brit butler or even Siegfried. And he did not look happy to see her.

Paige supposed they didn't get many visitors here. It's not as though any kids would be peddling cookies at this door. Maybe Mia had sent her here because it was where the family kept their drugged prisoners, the ones who were tortured, or worse yet, forced to listen to Linde's opera.

Paige cleared her throat. "Excuse me, but I'm looking for Siegfried," she said, her voice a mere squeak.

The man eyed her suspiciously. "How did you find this entrance? Do you realize you are trespassing on private property?" he asked in a threatening manner. Squat and beefy-necked, he resembled a movie thug.

Paige swallowed, her earlier fears replaced by visions of loaded guns. But her only alternative to this less-than-warm reception was to hike back up the cliff, and that realization made her square her shoulders.

"Mia sent me," she said. "To get Siegfried. For dinner."

"And just who are you?"

Paige told herself the guy wasn't menacing her, simply making conversation. "I'm the wedding planner," she said. As soon as the words left her mouth, Paige realized how ridiculous they sounded, especially considering that in her current condition she bore little resemblance to a professional of any kind, er, except maybe one.

She was standing barefoot and bedraggled, her hair a mess, and holding a broken shoe. And now this guy, who obviously didn't believe her, was going to shoot her.

At least she'd be out of her misery.

For a long moment, Paige wilted under the man's scrutiny, certain he was going to slam the door on her or worse. But then, somewhere behind him, she caught a glimpse of dark hair possibly more disheveled than her own.

And at this point, she didn't care what the Maitland heir

was: boy genius, recluse, gawky skateboarder, or rude billionaire. Leaning forward, Paige opened her mouth and yelled, in a very unbusinesslike manner.

"Siegfried!"

Siegfried halted in his steps and turned toward the sound of his name. He usually didn't notice when anyone called to him, but something about that voice made him look up. A woman was standing in the old doorway, and even though he hardly ever put names to faces and often forgot people entirely, she seemed familiar.

"It's Paige," she reminded him. "You knocked me down with your skateboard. Remember?"

Siegfried remembered all right. He remembered the feel of a soft, luscious body beneath his, for the first time in... well, too long. She had been pretty, too, with sleek, dark blond hair and green eyes.

Siegfried honed in on her from across the room and felt a jolt of recognition. Yes, that was her. But what was she doing here and now?

Although he hadn't asked the question aloud, she cleared her throat. "I've come to get you for dinner."

Siegfried stared in surprise. He couldn't recall the last time someone had dragged him to the dining room.

His mother had been a free spirit who hadn't particularly concerned herself with her children, and his father had been too busy for regularly scheduled meals. By the time Bebe stepped in, Siegfried's lax eating habits were ingrained.

Yet, suddenly, he was ravenously hungry. "Okay."

But Tad came between him and the woman. "I don't think she should be in here, sir. It's a restricted area."

Siegfried eyed the guard curiously. "Since when? Dad always let us come down here. Grandpa, too." Now, that had been fun because his grandfather had dabbled in explosives. Of course, the lab had looked different then, more homey and less sterile. Siegfried frowned.

"You are referring to family members, sir," Tad said. His

clipped speech reminded Siegfried of some kind of dog, though he wasn't sure which one. Never having owned a pet, he didn't know much about them.

"You've got company business going on here, some of it highly confidential."

Siegfried glanced toward the young woman hidden behind the guard. "I don't think she's a corporate spy."

But Tad shook his head. "You can't be sure, sir. And she could very well be a reporter. You know how often they have tried to infiltrate the compound."

Siegfried realized that Tad took his job a bit too seriously. He used words like "infiltrate" and "compound," just as though he were a government operative. Most of the time, Siegfried didn't notice, but now he found it annoying.

However, Bebe insisted they have some kind of security, if only to make sure Siegfried didn't blow up the house, even though he had assured her his work was not incendiary. And they had gone through plenty of guards before this one, employees being the bane of the Maitlands.

"Tad's a little overzealous," Siegfried explained, heading toward the visitor. What was her name?

"I'm just trying to do my job, sir," Tad said, positioning himself in front of the woman as if to keep Siegfried from her."I don't think the company—"

Although Siegfried was not very perceptive as far as human behavior went, even he could see a long argument coming. And nothing wasted more time than unnecessary debate, so he cut Tad off with a shrug.

"But I'm the CEO. So come on in," he said over Tad's shoulder.

The woman looked relieved as she stepped past the security guard. "Thank you! I was not going up that cliff again."

Paige. That was her name. Siegfried was surprised it came to him, but then, this woman was surprising. When she moved fully into view, he saw that she looked a little different. Some of her blond hair had fallen out of its knot in the back, so silky strands framed her face.

And she was even lovelier than he remembered, not all sharp cheekbones and stick thin, like so many women, but rounder, more friendly. But not fat, either. Just right.

She filled out the suit nicely, Siegfried thought as his gaze traveled lower. She had gorgeous legs and... bare feet, he realized, sucking in a deep breath. People ran around the house all the time with no shoes, but there was something about these particular bare feet that suffused him with heat.

Studying her closely, Siegfried catalogued everything about her from the dirt smudges on her skirt to the tiny mole above one eyebrow. Women usually ignored him, and he rarely noticed them in return, but this one had captured his attention more than once. He felt a surge of interest, the kind that came with a breakthrough in his work, a new invention or discovery.

The discovery of Paige.

"Of course, I'll need to get, uh, cleaned up before dinner," she said, drawing his gaze back to her face. She had flushed a delightful shade of pink. "Just for your information, there isn't really a path down here," she said, her voice tight.

"It doesn't get much use anymore," Siegfried said. He glanced at the footwear in her hand. "And I sure wouldn't try it in those shoes."

She appeared to be annoyed at his observation, and Siegfried cursed his poor social skills. Usually, he didn't even bother trying. But he had a feeling, the kind he had learned not to ignore when pursuing an idea, that this woman would be worth the effort.

However, since Paige was unlike any of the other Maitland discoveries, Siegfried had no idea how to proceed. He was accustomed to dealing with challenges, solving puzzles, and managing strategies involving his work, but this was a living, breathing female. And as he faced her, all he could think was: now what?

CHAPTER FIVE

Paige was so relieved to be inside and past the menacing security guard that she was tempted to throw herself at Siegfried's rumpled form and proclaim him her hero—until she realized he was the reason she was here in the first place.

And she couldn't imagine sitting down to discuss the proposed wedding in his underground facility with its freezing temperatures and harsh lighting. Paige wasn't even sure there were chairs as she looked around the space, its bright white unrelieved except for huge monitors.

Modern and clean, it was not the sort of place the old wooden door had led her to expect—a secret lab with the bubbling potions and giant electrodes of Dr. Frankenstein's creepy lair. And yet... were those body parts atop those tables?

Paige blinked at the eerie collection of white limbs, black hands, and blank faces that resembled that hockey-mask killer from the movies. Maybe the cliff outside wasn't so bad after all, she thought, frantically trying to don one of Zoe's broken shoes.

"Here, let me help you." Siegfried stepped forward, dark hair flopping into his eyes.

Paige didn't know whether he was going to try to fix the shoes or use her corpse for spare parts, but before she could object he swung her up into his arms. Although Paige squeaked in surprise, he began carrying her across the room just as though she weighed nothing, which definitely wasn't true.

She protested that she could walk, and the bullying security guy followed behind protesting that she *should* walk. But Siegfried paid them no heed, which was kind of cool and manly. Suddenly, the guy didn't seem like a teenage skateboarder, but a full-fledged adult male with the strength and broad shoulders to prove it.

Not that it mattered, Paige told herself. She was here for a business opportunity, not to be carried off by Siegfried Maitland. She drew in a deep breath to clear her head, but instead sucked down a lungful of that good-guy smell she remembered from earlier.

With her last remaining wits, Paige wondered whether she really had hit her head. Or maybe she was dizzy from the unnatural elevation. After all, when had a man ever carried her in his arms before?

Never. And Paige was beginning to think maybe she ought to enjoy herself because who knew when it would happen again? She was way too busy to date, and there weren't many guys who would sweep her off her feet even in the heat of romance, let alone just to be gentlemanly.

Only an eccentric like Siegfried could be counted upon for such heroics. But he also might drop her at any moment, especially if something more interesting turned up, like a skateboard.

Thankfully, the offending object was not in sight as Siegfried strode across the room, but it did look like they were heading toward a blank wall. Okay, so maybe it was time to make him let her down, she thought, remembering his lunatic tendencies.

But just as Paige opened her mouth, she realized that there was something ahead. Although Siegfried did nothing, cleverly hidden doors slid open, and he stepped inside what appeared to be an elevator, with her still cradled in his arms. And he wasn't even huffing. Did the guy work out, or what?

Someone was definitely huffing. Tad looked like he wanted to step in the elevator with them, just to make sure Paige didn't overpower the boy genius as soon as they were alone. Hmm. Maybe *he* would overpower *her?* A girl could always hope.

But when the mysterious doors slid back into place, Siegfried didn't make a move or say anything. In fact, Paige began to feel ridiculous as he stared straight ahead while they traveled upward.

"You can put me down now," she said, stifling a baser instinct to remain right where she was. "I'm sure the floor is fine." A peek downward revealed that it was parquet and polished to a sheen. And she was already feeling warmer, although that might be because of the incredibly delightful heat of the body she was pressed against.

"Oh, yeah. Of course," Siegfried mumbled as he let her slide down his body to her feet.

Gawky? Maybe. But geeky? Uh, no. The boy genius was all male: tall, strong, and gorgeous. They stood still, nearly touching, for one long moment while all sorts of wild ideas formed in her normally reasonable brain. Then the elevator doors opened.

"Ah, Ms. Porter. There you are." The sound of a British accent shook Paige from her daze. She turned and blinked at the butler.

"I believe this is yours," he said, presenting the large handbag she had left on the terrace.

"And who is this you have with you?" the butler asked. "Oh, Mr. Siegfried. It's been so long since you've dined with the family that I'd forgotten you lived here."

Just as Paige was digesting that bit of sarcasm, Godfrey turned his full attention on her. She realized what she had forgotten in Siegfried's arms: that she looked like a mess and was barefoot and holding a broken shoe. The blood rushed to her face.

"Did we have another accident, Ms. Porter?" the butler asked, his white brows lifting.

Was he mocking her? Paige gaped in astonishment as his gaze traveled to the heels dangling from her fingers.

"Do you require some new footwear?" he asked. Although the servant's tone revealed nothing, there was something about his deadpan expression that told Paige he was looking down his proper British nose at her.

Straightening, she donned her most businesslike demeanor. "No, thank you. I'm fine."

With as much dignity as possible, she slipped on the shoes,

teetering in the one and hobbling along on the other, its missing heel clutched in her hand. Darting a glance at the butler, she lifted her own brows, as though daring him to say more.

He bowed slightly. "Very good then," he said. "You are awaited in the dining room. If you would follow me?"

Already rattled by Godfrey, Paige was annoyed to see that Siegfried had moved on without her. She hadn't gone to this much trouble to watch him slip away. And how else was she to explain her bedraggled appearance? Shuffling to catch up with him, Paige grabbed his arm in a death grip.

"We are going to dinner. Remember?" she asked.

"Oh, yeah. Right," he said, looking down at her. And then he smiled.

When those luscious lips curved upward, Paige's irritation disappeared, along with all the breath in her lungs. This guy was really good-looking. And warm. And genuine.

The smile reached his eyes and made Paige's heart pound in response, which, in turn, set warning bells to buzzing in her head. She had but a minute to remind herself that she was here strictly for business before Godfrey stepped in front of them and swung open a pair of massive mahogany doors.

"Dinner is served," he announced with his usual gravity, while Paige blinked at the scene before her.

She had pictured the wealthy Maitlands dressing for the meal in elegant formalwear and chatting over drinks with the city's movers and shakers. But it was a ragtag bunch who were already seated at a huge table in the cavernous room, a kind of creepy Tudor hall with dark paneling, dim lighting, and hunting paintings gracing the walls.

Somehow, it just wasn't how Paige had envisioned one of the city's first families gathering. Although the china and crystal and linens obviously were the finest, the assemblage was not quite as glittering. And they were all talking at once. Loudly.

"Ah, Paige! There you are!" Bebe's voice rose from her place at one end of the massive piece of furniture.

The babble died down to a low murmur, and Paige realized how she must look: battered, bruised, and clinging to the heir apparent. Clearing her throat, Paige prepared to explain, but Bebe didn't give her a chance.

"Paige has brought Siegfried!" she said in a breathless tone. "See, I told you how helpful she would be."

Then everyone started speaking at once. Thankfully, none of the talk seemed to be about Paige's appearance. Siegfried was the general topic of discussion as he moved to the end of the table, where an empty chair must stand in reserve for him. Unfortunately, there were no seats nearby, and no one offered to make a place for Paige. Why should they? It was not as though she and Siegfried were together. In fact, he seemed to have forgotten her already, and Paige tried to ignore the way he ignored her. Again.

Grabbing the nearest open spot, Paige told herself she didn't care where she was as long as she got a chance to meet the bride and groom. And as she sat down, she glanced around the table curiously. Although she didn't see any obvious candidates for matrimony, she had met some pretty odd couples before, so she didn't rule anyone out.

Linde was there, with Lorenzo beside her, but Mia Anderson was notably absent, which probably was a good thing. After her trip to the lab at Mia's direction, Paige was in no mood to deal with the spoiled heiress.

However, the girl at least would have been a familiar face. Paige couldn't help wondering who all these people were. Extended family? Friends?

"Where's Lila?" a man asked her.

"Lila doesn't serve on Tuesdays," a woman across the table replied. "Her Goth group meets in the evening."

Goth group? Paige reached for her wineglass as soon as it was filled by a nervous-looking young woman in a white apron.

A sudden jostling made her glass tip and the liquid slosh precariously. Luckily, the man on her right was ready with a napkin, so she didn't add a red stain to her already ruined suit.

"I'm Uncle Otto," the older man said in a German accent so thick it sounded real, as opposed to some of the more suspect ones she'd heard here.

"Paige Porter. I'm a wedding planner."

"Ah, the wedding!" he said.

A chorus of sighs greeted his words. And soon Paige was inundated with questions and suggestions from everyone in her immediate vicinity. Thankfully, none were as outlandish as the opera theme, but there were some wild ones.

Far from the quiet repast among politicians and philanthropists Paige had expected, the meal was more like feeding time at the zoo. And some of the guests looked as if they had wandered in off the streets. The girl who was serving was new, and when she spilled wine on someone's lap and burst into tears, Bebe insisted she take a seat at the table and join in.

"We'll pour our own wine," someone suggested jovially.

Paige never did find out the identities of all the guests. The woman on her left, an elderly lady no bigger than a bird, ate prodigious amounts of food and rebuffed all attempts at conversation.

And Uncle Otto turned out to be no one's uncle. He had been someone's pen pal and having arrived for a visit, he had simply stayed on—for thirty years. He claimed to do odd jobs around the estate, including repairs necessitated by the experiments Siegfried's father and grandfather had conducted.

Glancing around, Paige felt as though she had stepped right into one of the old screwball comedies. But as much as she enjoyed vintage movies, she didn't want to live in one.

She tried to focus on business, but Uncle Otto said the engaged couple were not present. He claimed they rarely joined the other diners because Mack was working on a new painting.

Mack? And Flosshilde? Paige could just picture the wedding invitations. "Is he a well-known artist?" she asked.

"Oh no. He is the young one, the newcomer. His work has never been shown," Uncle Otto said.

"Have you seen it?" Paige asked, curious now.

"Oh no. No one has!"

"But what about his teachers, mentors? Surely, he went to art classes," Paige said.

"No," Otto said, with a proud smile. "He is entirely unschooled."

Paige blinked as her cynicism kicked in. How many times had Zoe accused her of being too jaded? But as someone who made her living off the dreams of couples likely to divorce, it was hard to keep her pessimism in check.

And now she couldn't help wondering whether this Mack, untrained and unseen, was really a painter or just a guy who was taking advantage of the Maitlands. A glance around the table told her it was not that difficult to worm one's way into the family circle.

But everyone did background checks these days, Paige reminded herself, even brides-to-be, and surely people with as much money as the Maitlands would be wary of opportunists. And yet... Paige's gaze wandered toward the head of the household.

She wasn't sure what Siegfried's position was, but she couldn't imagine him taking an active role in anything except skateboarding and secret labs. It was hard to believe the guy had carried her in his arms, she thought with a frown.

Obviously, he'd lost all interest in her now. But he didn't seem to be engaging with anyone else, either. He ate as though distracted, his prodigious mind apparently elsewhere.

No wonder the guy skipped meals, if this was the Maitlands' idea of a quiet dinner at home, Paige thought. She began to feel a bit guilty for dragging him from his sanctuary.

Perhaps he'd prefer a more laid-back setting, Paige mused, entertaining visions of intimate suppers on the terrace or in one of the many other rooms. Flushing, Paige dismissed those thoughts and tried to concentrate on business.

Since the bridal couple was nowhere to be seen, her only course was to approach Bebe about meeting them. As conversation died down and some of the diners began to exit, Paige kept a wary eye on her hostess. And when Bebe rose to her feet, Paige seized her opportunity.

Leaving Zoe's shoes under the table, she hurried toward the older woman, trying her best to look professional in her bare feet and grubby suit.

"Thank you for inviting me to share your meal. It was delightful," Paige said. "However, I was hoping I might have a chance to talk with your granddaughter and her future husband."

"Oh dear," Bebe said, glancing about as though she just now realized the couple wasn't at the table. "I sent a message up to the studio requesting that they come to dinner to meet you. But when the muse is upon Mack, he doesn't like to be interrupted by such mundane things as sustenance."

Perhaps they lived on their love, Paige thought—or room service. "Well, could I just speak with your granddaughter?"

"Oh no." Bebe shook her head. "They are inseparable. Mack says that Flosshilde is his inspiration, and he simply cannot work when she isn't there."

Paige's smile remained fixed, but her patience had reached its end. As much as she had enjoyed her little trip down the rabbit hole, she couldn't hang around Wonderland forever, hoping for a chance encounter with the mysterious duo.

She had other responsibilities, including contracted weddings, and she couldn't put them on hold while hanging out for the possibility of this one. "Well, I'm sorry that I'm unable to fulfill your needs," Paige said.

"Oh, but you do, my dear!" Bebe said, looking surprised. "You are just what we were looking for."

Paige eyed her in confusion. "But what about the clients?"

"We are your clients, dear," Bebe said, with an indulgent smile. "Everyone approves, so you are hired."

Everyone who? "And the bride-to-be?" Paige asked.

"Oh," Bebe said, waving her hand in a gesture of unconcern. "I guess you'll just have to come back tomorrow, unless you would like to spend the night?"

Paige blinked, shook her head, and made her escape before

things could get any weirder. Eccentric? Zoe didn't know the meaning of the word.

"You what?" Zoe dropped the gold netting she was gathering into bows and turned to stare at Paige. "Don't tell me you refused an invitation to stay at the Maitland estate?"

Paige shrugged.

"Don't tell me."

"All right, I won't," Paige said. Having successfully put off the topic for days, she finally had been forced to cough up some details to compensate for Zoe's ruined shoes.

"And I like the silver better," Paige said, pointing to the gossamer material.

"Wait until you see this in the candlelight, though," Zoe said. Then her brows lowered. "Don't change the subject. Are you crazy?"

"No. In fact, I was probably the only sane person there," Paige said. "I assume that's how all the crazies ended up there. They were invited to spend the night and never left. It's like a dog pound for people, with Bebe Maitland making the rescues."

"If that's what you want to call it, then sign me up as a homeless wannabe," Zoe said. "They probably have gold fixtures in the bathrooms and handmade Egyptian sheets."

"And maybe I'd rather have chrome and flannel, thank you," Paige said. She couldn't explain the strangeness of the place to Zoe. It was like being invited into Wackyland, where everything was just a little off. "Believe me, when you go up there, you enter another dimension—the twilight zone."

"Another dimension of luxury. How hard can it be having servants wait on you hand and foot?" Zoe asked.

Paige remembered the Maitland employees—menacing, inept, rude—and she snorted. "It's not quite the paradise you imagine."

Although there was a certain appeal to the place and its owner, Siegfried had disappeared after dinner without even a look in her direction, and Paige wasn't an orphan for Bebe to take in. She was a professional with a business to run, and the last time she checked, sleepovers were not part of her duties. Unlike Zoe, she was perfectly satisfied with her own apartment, small, quiet, and normal.

Zoe shook her head in disgust, her burnished curls bouncing slightly with the movement. "Well, at least you got the wedding assignment. Maybe they'll invite you to stay again. And you can bring me along."

Zoe stood back to admire her work as sunlight caught the netting, making it sparkle like a film of jewels. Although Paige possessed the organizational skills and business acumen that made the enterprise a success, Zoe had a romantic vision that gave an exquisite aura to even the smallest of their weddings.

Together, they were unstoppable.

"So what date are we talking about? We'll need to schedule everything else around this one," Zoe said.

Date? Paige had no date. She didn't even have a bride-to-be. All she had were more invitations to the nuthouse. "Who knows?" she asked with a sigh. "I keep calling up there, but the engaged couple won't even talk to me."

Despite an unaccountable desire to see the boy genius again, Paige had stuck to business, insisting that she couldn't come out to the estate unless Flosshilde was going to be available. She did not want a repeat of her last adventure.

However, after several days of refusing Bebe's requests for brunch, lunch, and dinner, without a promise of a meeting, Paige had begun to give up hope.

"The rich are different," Zoe said. "You have to dance to their tune. Why aren't you up there kissing butt and eating gourmet meals?"

"Because I don't have the time for it," Paige said. She had gotten where she was by focusing on her goals—and the bottom line—and she wasn't going to invest any more of her energy without some kind of commitment.

"Well, I think I could make the time," Zoe said, "especially for one of the Bay Area's most eligible bachelors."

Paige frowned. Although Zoe had peppered her with questions about Siegfried, she had volunteered little. After all, the boy genius was reclusive for a reason, and she was a businesswoman, not a gossip columnist.

And as much as she appreciated her friend's search for a rich husband, offering up the clients was not an option. Zoe was a wonderful girl, but she was on a mission, and Siegfried, from what Paige had seen, would be no match for her.

"He's not the one getting married," Paige said. She felt oddly protective of the guy, who had a lost-little-boy quality about him, probably because he couldn't even remember to feed himself. She wondered, suddenly, if he was eating, and then shook her head. It was no concern of hers. If she had been a little dazed by his gallant act of carrying her across the concrete, she put it down to her injuries sustained when he had knocked her down.

"Yeah, but he could be a side benefit to the job," Zoe said, interrupting her thoughts.

"He's too young for you," Paige said, suddenly annoyed at the course of the conversation.

"Hello?" Zoe paused to give her a look. "He's the same age you are."

Paige sucked in a breath. Okay, so he wasn't a teenager after all. If she was relieved at the news, it was only because she wouldn't have to deal with some underage billionaire.

"And so what if he's a bit of geek, from what I hear?" Zoe asked. "I wouldn't mind."

"He's not a geek," Paige said.

Zoe's sudden, curious glance made her turn away.

"So what is he, then?" Zoe asked.

Paige cleared her throat and straightened a satin sash. "He's very smart and... private."

"Hmm. Sounds delightfully mysterious," Zoe said in a throaty way that made Paige bristle.

"Look, I'll handle the Maitlands," Paige said. "You work your magic, and I'll take care of business."

And that included Siegfried.

CHAPTER SIX

When Paige stood in front of the Maitland mansion for the second time, she was determined to focus on her job. She wasn't going to gawk at the genius. Or be played by the mean-girl heiress. Or be sucked into the general weirdness.

This trip was strictly business. For a moment, she even let herself imagine the ultimate dream: a franchise, her own wedding planning services in all the big cities and Paige as CEO. It was her singular vision.

So why did Siegfried Maitland keep popping into the picture? Paige frowned just as the door swung open to reveal the butler in all his stately glory. But Paige wasn't surprised when he glanced toward her feet.

"I see you are properly shod today, Ms. Porter," he observed, as if congratulating her on the achievement.

"Are you mocking me, Godfrey?" Paige asked. She was beginning to believe that behind his stoic demeanor lay an acerbic wit the butler honed on everyone, including his employers.

"Certainly not, miss," he answered, but when he turned, Paige thought she saw his lips twitch. "Miss Flosshilde will meet you in the salon."

"I thought she never left the studio," Paige said, moving beside him. "I was hoping to catch a glimpse of Mack's work."

"The artist's loft is over the garages," Godfrey said. "And Mr. Mack keeps everything locked up there. He rarely allows visitors."

I'll bet, Paige thought to herself. Locked doors or not, the butler probably knew everything about everyone in the household, and she was tempted to ask him more about this Mack. But she suspected there was a limit to Godfrey's candor.

Putting the groom's motives out of her mind, Paige followed Godfrey to the salon. It was a lovely room, with the drapes pulled to allow more light and gorgeous ocean views. The walls were a pale yellow, and the furniture consisted of English cottage pieces and graceful antiques, a far cry from the decor in other areas of the house.

But if there was a noticeable lack of medieval furnishings, there seemed to be an absence of occupants, too. Were the Maitlands up to their usual tricks? Paige turned slowly only to halt in surprise when she spotted a young woman curled up in a high-backed chair.

Bare feet tucked under her and long hair falling into her face, she looked even younger than Siegfried and about as socially backward. Paige swallowed her surprise and stepped forward.

"Hello? You must be the bride-to-be," she said. It was not hard to tell that the woman was a Maitland. These two sisters and their brother shared a certain likeness, although Siegfried was the best looking of the three. Or, at least, it would seem that way to a woman, Paige amended. Any woman. *Not just her.*

Paige smiled as she reached out to shake Flosshilde's hand. Despite her absence at meals, the girl must be eating, for she shared her sister's build, even though she was more Paige's height than Linde's. But she certainly did not share the diva's demeanor, shrinking away after the first tentative grip.

Paige tried to peer through the hair to see the face better. Was this girl even old enough to marry? And just how old was Mack? She pictured a middle-aged bully straight out of a mafia movie, running roughshod all over the girl.

It was none of her business, Paige told herself as she settled into a nearby seat. Approval of the groom was not a part of her service, and just because the guy had an unusual name and occupation did not make him a villain. Everyone in this house had a weird name, and there were some pretty weird vocations, too.

Paige smiled encouragingly at the girl. Maybe she simply was shy, which was understandable, if she'd been home-schooled like her brother.

"I'm so glad that we were able to meet," Paige said."I've gotten lots of input from your family, but I'm eager to hear what you have in mind."

Flosshilde mumbled something that Paige couldn't make out. Perhaps Linde was the only one of the siblings blessed with the power of articulate speech?

"Did you want some refreshments, miss?"

The voice, coming through loud and clear, obviously did not belong to Flosshilde. Turning her head, Paige blinked as she came face-to-face with a young woman dressed all in black with short, midnight hair rising in spikes all over her head, and a face that was dead white. She looked like she had stepped straight out of a midnight showing of *Rocky Horror*.

"Some fruit juice, Miss Flosshilde?" the girl asked. Completely oblivious to Paige's shock, she smiled, which made the bolt in her lip bob. Paige marveled at the multiple piercings, chains, and black nails until she realized this must be the servant who met with a Goth group on Tuesday nights.

"Lila?" Paige whispered.

"Yes, miss," she said. "A diet cola for you?"

Paige nodded. "Thanks." She had no clue where the Maitlands got their help, but they obviously didn't have a strict dress code. She turned back toward Flosshilde, who couldn't have looked more different in a long dress, with a toe ring adorning one of her delicate feet.

Drawing in a deep breath, Paige reminded herself not to get sucked into the weirdness. "Tell me some of your ideas," she urged. In many cases, the brides had every detail already in mind. Others were more vague, and it was Paige's job to offer different options.

Once a date was set, the first big decision was the venue. There were a myriad of choices in the Bay Area, from elegant hotels to Victorian mansions to chic modern museums. Outdoor gardens abounded, including island spots and breathtaking views, and water weddings were celebrated on everything from moored antique vessels to dashing yachts.

Although destination weddings were growing more popular, Paige was hoping to work locally, the better to showcase her own talents. But it all depended upon the atmosphere the bride was looking for, the number of guests, and the amount of money available, which, Paige assumed, was not going to be a problem.

Of course, with a little work, Flosshilde had the ideal location right in her own backyard, but Paige wanted to hear her out before making any suggestions.

"I don't know. I haven't really thought about it," the girl mumbled. She hung her head and fiddled with one of the many rings on her hands.

"Do you envision yourself outdoors or inside?" Paige asked.

"It doesn't really matter."

Paige's eyes widened. She had spoken with a lot of brides, some with a near-psychotic attention to detail and others with grandiose plans that would be impossible to implement. But not one single woman had ever said that something *didn't matter.*

Paige drew a deep breath. "Hilde. May I call you Hilde?"

The girl looked up, as though startled, and then smiled, a reaction that transformed her face from merely pretty to striking. "Hilde. I like that," she murmured.

Paige nodded. Now, perhaps they could get down to business. "How many guests do you plan to invite?"

The flash of good humor was gone, and a sullen expression descended. Hilde reminded Paige of nothing so much as a teenager backed into a corner. How old was she? Paige wondered. Did she really want to get married? Did she *have* to?

Perhaps the girl just didn't approve of Bebe's choice of planner. Sometimes, personality differences came into play, and Zoe had to step in. But Paige recoiled at the thought. She felt a sudden, fierce possessiveness toward the Maitland nuptials. And besides, this girl hadn't even given her a chance.

"If you're worried about our service, let me assure you that we can do almost anything you have in mind," Paige said.

Hilde shook her head, still fiddling with her rings. "It's just that Mack and I are not really into that whole thing," she explained.

Paige stiffened. What thing? The show Paige was responsible for staging? As Paige struggled for a reply, Hilde lifted her head, oblivious to her guest's dismay. Then she uttered the *coup de grace*—a few simple words that struck Paige like a knife through the heart, destroying all her hopes and dreams in one breath.

"I don't really want a fancy wedding."

By the time Hilde left the room to return to her fiancé, Paige had recovered from her initial shock and made some progress. They had set a date, at least, and Hilde had agreed to an acceptable number of guests, considering her family, their position in the community, and her grandmother's wishes.

If it wasn't quite the wedding Paige had envisioned, well, size wasn't as important as class, anyway. And style. And a three-day event, though popular among the wealthy, wasn't really necessary. A single ceremony could be just as impressive. At least that's what Paige kept telling herself.

Although she had suggested several different venues, Hilde seemed most comfortable with hosting the event here at the estate. The Maitland home had a certain cachet, and the views were priceless. But a team of gardeners would be needed to get the place into shape, and Paige made a memo in her phone to price some services.

The wheels were already turning in her head, making Paige anxious to get with Zoe, but Godfrey had instructed her to wait for Bebe. In full professional mode, Paige hoped that her productive day would not degenerate with the arrival of the family matriarch. As much as she liked the woman, Paige was determined not to stay any longer.

"Ah, Paige!" Bebe arrived in a cloud of expensive perfume and stepped forward to press a kiss to her cheek. Never having known a grandmother or extended family of her own, Paige felt a sudden surge of yearning that she promptly suppressed. *Stick to business,* she reminded herself.

"So, did you have a satisfactory meeting with Flosshilde?" Bebe asked, gesturing for Paige to take a seat.

Paige nodded. She carefully laid out Hilde's decisions, hoping that none would be vetoed by Bebe, and let out a sigh of relief when they were not.

"Oh, I am so glad we are to have the ceremony here! That will be utterly delightful. However, I'm afraid we have been getting a bit overgrown since our gardener quit," the older woman said.

"Don't worry. I'll take care of that."

"Oh, would you, dear? We do so need a groundskeeper again. Hire at least one full-timer, please."

Paige blinked. She hadn't meant to look for permanent employees, but she could, while taking on some extra workers for the preparations.

"All right," Paige said.

"Oh, thank you! I knew I could count on you," Bebe said. "Now that you have begun the planning, you do realize what will be your most important responsibility?" The older woman leaned forward, eyeing Paige expectantly.

Was this a test? Usually, coordinating the caterers, the flowers, and the musicians were high on the list of priorities. But for some people, it was preservation of the memories. "The videographer?" Paige said.

"No, dear. Your most important task will be to give everyone their assignments, get them into their clothes, and make sure they are in place at the proper time. As you may have noticed, our household is a bit undirected. So, *you* must direct. Especially Siegfried."

For some reason, the thought of directing the boy genius wasn't quite as objectionable as it sounded. But Paige was not witless. She knew that if Bebe was warning her, she would face quite a challenge. She had only to remember the other night's dinner to get an idea of what lay ahead.

But she kept the Holy Grail of weddings firmly in mind and gritted her teeth. If necessary, she would employ "minders" to monitor each member of the family taking part in the ceremony.

"Of course. I'm sure I can manage," Paige said.

"I know you will," Bebe said, reaching out to pat her hand. "Now, speaking of Siegfried, you will need to get with him on all your plans since he will be handling the financial end."

Paige drew in a deep breath and chose her next words carefully. "I understand, but Siegfried is not really interested in discussing the wedding. Perhaps, we should just proceed, and then I can present him with an estimate?"

"Oh no, that won't do," Bebe said, shaking her head. "I called down to the office, and Willow assured me that he will be able to meet with you today."

"Today?" Paige echoed. She had not scheduled anything else, just in case she met with problems here, but she was not prepared to run to Siegfried's office on a moment's notice. In fact, she couldn't imagine him in an office. Didn't he work down in the secret lab?

But Bebe was already rising to her feet, as though the discussion were over. "In fact, you should probably get going," she said, pausing to glance at her diamond-studded watch. "I can have Arthur drive you."

"Now?" Paige didn't bother to hide her dismay.

"Yes, dear. As head of the family, Siegfried must approve all the expenditures," Bebe said.

Paige found that hard to believe, especially since the guy wasn't allowed to carry money. Yet he ran a company, didn't he? So Paige swallowed her protest, her unwillingness overcome by the thought of the high-society wedding, the accompanying fat paycheck, and a certain unwitting anticipation at the prospect of seeing the guy again.

"All right," Paige said, knowing she had been manipulated once again by Bebe, a master of the craft. "Where do I go?"

CHAPTER SEVEN

Not wanting to leave her precious car at the family zoo, er, estate, Paige insisted on driving herself, which meant finding a parking space down off Market. The building that housed The Maitland Company was easy to locate, but getting in was another story.

Even though Bebe had called ahead, Paige thought she was going to have to undergo fingerprinting just to get past security, which made her wonder about the nature of the Maitland family business. What did the company do, handle top-secret government projects? Paige glanced about curiously, but the understated lobby told her nothing.

Once she was approved, the beautiful but bored-looking receptionist waved her upstairs toward the elevator. And on the upper floor, Paige found herself in another spacious, well-appointed lobby overseen by another gorgeous female. This one was Ms. Feagin, according to her nameplate, and she seemed just as bored as her counterpart below.

"And which Mr. Maitland did you wish to see?" she asked, her incredibly long nails poised over some sort of elaborate phone system.

Paige blinked. "There's more than one?" She couldn't imagine anyone else in the world like Siegfried.

"Yes. If Blake told you he was the CEO and president, I'm sorry to disappoint you. He's not," Ms. Feagin said without glancing up at Paige.

"Blake? Who's Blake? I'm here to see Siegfried," Paige said.

At that, Ms. Feagin gave Paige her full attention. "Siegfried?" she echoed, as if that were unusual. Did the guy go by another name here?

"Yes. Siegfried Maitland," Paige said. ""Who's Blake?" she asked again, wondering if there was some brother she didn't know about.

"Blake's a cousin," the receptionist said in a tone of dismissal that made her low opinion of the man clear. Maybe he was a difficult boss, though Paige couldn't imagine Siegfried being an easy one. He probably got lost going to the restroom and disappeared for days on end.

"Oh, I'm sorry. I didn't even know Blake existed," Paige said.

Ms. Feagin laughed, a husky, infectious sound that made Paige smile. "Better not let him know that."

Paige nodded and filed the information away for future reference, just in case the infamous cousin was tagged as a groomsman. "I'll keep that in mind."

"So you're here for Mr. Siegfried Maitland?" Ms. Feagin asked, lifting her dark brows. "He usually doesn't see anyone."

Maybe he wouldn't see her, either, Paige thought, with a sense of relief. But that was followed by disappointment, probably because she didn't want to come back. It certainly wasn't because she wanted to meet with the boy genius, who might not talk to her even if she did get inside his office.

While Paige frowned, Ms. Feagin spoke softly into her headset, then shook her head, a look of amazement on her face.

"Well, Ms. Porter, it appears you are free to enter the inner sanctum," she said. She paused. "Before you do, I probably ought to warn you that Mr. Maitland's assistant is a bit different."

"Naturally," Paige said. Considering the estate employees, she was prepared for anything from a dominatrix to a trained monkey. But from the looks of the people here, the company seemed to be staffed with a different type.

"Let me guess. Is she a supermodel?"

Ms. Feagin laughed. "No, she's far more... Zen."

"Of course," Paige said. "How else could she work for him?"

Ms. Feagin laughed again, a whoop that turned the heads of others in the lobby. "You got that right. He couldn't keep an assistant until Willow arrived. She just doesn't let him get to her, but..." Ms. Feagin let her words trail off, as though waiting for encouragement.

"Yes?" Paige prodded. It was her job to know as much as she could about her clients, wasn't it? And Paige couldn't help her sudden, fierce curiosity about the Maitland heir.

Ms. Feagin leaned closer. "It might be better if someone could get him to his meetings."

"I'm sure you're right," Paige said. But that kind of feat probably would try even a yogi. "Thank you, Ms. Feagin, you've been a great help."

"No problem. It's Latasha. I'll see you around?"

Paige nodded. She'd be around until the wedding, though probably not here. She couldn't imagine returning to The Maitland Company offices any time soon, but it was always good to know the employees, whether the business was a florist shop or a huge corporation. And everyone was a potential customer.

Siegfried's assistant, another lovely young woman, was waiting for her, and Paige wondered if there were any men at all employed here, beyond the Maitlands and the security guys. She frowned. Did the boy genius have a thing for these model types? Paige shook her head. Well, she certainly wasn't tall or skinny enough to qualify.

Willow was both. A pale, slender beauty with wild strawberry-blond hair, she wore a placid expression at odds with her mane. In fact, Willow looked so serene that Paige wondered whether she was on some mood-altering meds. Had working for Siegfried turned her to drink or drugs? Paige could easily imagine the possibility.

Putting on her business face, Paige stepped forward. "Hello. I'm here to see Mr. Maitland."

"Yes. Just a moment," the assistant said. But instead of buzzing Paige in, she walked over to the office door and slid some sort of key card through the security pad.

She turned to meet Paige's questioning look and gave her a rueful smile. "I locked him in the office."

"What?" Paige's voice went up an octave.

"That's the only way to be certain he'd stay until you got

here."

Paige was outraged. The head of the company was locked in his own office like some Alzheimer's patient. She felt a swift surge of protectiveness that made her want to fire the redhead on the spot. The only thing that kept her from speaking up was the knowledge that what happened here was none of her business.

Still, she was determined to say something to Siegfried about it. But when she stepped inside his office, she was struck dumb. Not many people would complain about being a prisoner here.

One entire wall was nothing except windows, with a view that stunned her. The light gave a golden glow to the interior, the carpet was obscenely thick, and the furniture nothing but the finest mahogany.

But the massive desk was unoccupied. Had Siegfried somehow escaped? Paige fervently hoped the windows did not open. She glanced about, a bit wildly, before she finally spotted him.

Oblivious to the luxury that surrounded him, he was in the corner hunched over the keyboard of a high-tech computer, its huge flat screen displaying all sorts of diagrams.

He looked like a nerd in paradise, and yet somehow Paige's heart lurched at the sight of him. His dark hair needed a trim, and she had the craziest desire to move behind him and stroke it. His hair, that is. Or maybe even his broad back encased in a baggy cotton shirt. It looked warm to the touch.

"Siegfried?" His name came out a whisper, and Paige cleared her throat. She spoke again, louder, and when he didn't respond, she moved toward him. Trying to gain his attention—and keep it—was always a frustrating effort.

But then he swung around, his face registering his surprise at her presence. Paige couldn't tell if the wide eyes meant he was glad or horrified to see her. And before she could decide, he stumbled to his feet, knocking over a pile of post-bound papers in the process.

As she watched him fumbling to retrieve them, Paige's heart lurched again. Or maybe it melted. Hardening herself against whatever her insides were doing, she walked forward to help him clean up the mess.

But when she knelt down to pick up some of the volumes, he froze. Did he expect her to do it all? Had he hurt himself?

Paige glanced up only to find him staring at her. More specifically, he was staring at her legs, where her skirt had ridden up to reveal most of her thigh.

Paige knew she ought to be amused or flattered, but instead her heart began pounding like a hammer. And in an even crazier reaction, she was seized by an urge to pull the guy down to the floor and show him anything he wanted to see.

It was totally unprofessional. Clearing her throat, Paige tried to tug at the hem of her skirt, but her precarious position rebelled, and suddenly, she was off balance. Literally.

Now she looked like an idiot, falling backward, her legs up in the air as she sputtered in embarrassment. Another guy might have laughed or taken the opportunity to join her on the lush carpeting, but not Siegfried. He was too much the gentleman to do either.

Paige didn't know whether she was disappointed or not when he stood over her and held out a hand to help her rise. It seemed way too much like a replay of the other day, without the good parts—like his warm body lying atop hers.

"Are you all right?"

"Yes," Paige mumbled as she was pulled to her feet. She couldn't decide whether Siegfried Maitland just naturally wrought havoc, like some kind of electrical storm, or if his own clumsiness was contagious. Maybe the guy really should be locked away.

"You don't have to help. I'll, uh, get someone in here to put the papers in order," he said, gesturing toward the materials littering his office.

Obviously, he was not going to comment on what just happened, which was probably a good thing. Paige smoothed her skirt and resolved to get back to business. "Bebe sent me to discuss the wedding."

At her words, the boy genius lifted his brows in surprise, as though she were proposing to him. Her heart thumped ridiculously at the thought.

"Hilde's?" Paige prompted. "Your sister?"

"Oh, yeah. Of course," he said. Although the information seemed to register, it didn't hold his interest, as evidenced by his next words. "Do you want to go skydiving?"

The question had Paige wondering whether she had hit her head when she fell. Again. Was it her, or was it Siegfried? He looked all right, better than all right, in fact, so maybe she had just misunderstood him.

"You want to jump out of a plane at your sister's wedding?"

"No. Of course not," he said. The disclaimer was accompanied by a curving of luscious lips that made Paige forget whatever nonsense was coming out of them. Sometimes, the guy just looked so good.

"I thought maybe we could get out of the office," he said, dismissing the lush accommodations with a gesture.

"To go sky diving?" Paige's voice came out as a squeak. The most good-looking guy in the world couldn't get her to jump out of a plane.

And besides, she was here on business, which couldn't be coherently discussed at twelve thousand feet. She shook her head. "I don't think so."

At her refusal, he looked so surprised and sort of lost that Paige felt her heart lurch again. She told herself that his disappointment had more to do with escaping his expensive prison than with keeping her company, but still...

"We could go to lunch," she said. "Have you eaten?"

That was a stupid question. Siegfried paused as though he had to stop to consider his answer, and Paige realized he probably hadn't ingested anything since she had forced him to go to dinner the other night. With a surge of annoyance, she wondered just how much Willow was paid and why she couldn't at least make sure her boss didn't starve to death when she locked him in his office.

Shaking his head, Siegfried looked at her and nodded. "Yeah, that sounds good," he said, as though she had floated some kind of innovative idea.

For a moment, Paige let herself imagine a late lunch or early supper at one of the city's finest restaurants on the arm of the Maitland heir. But a glance at her companion told her they wouldn't be admitted to any place too exclusive. Someone had neglected to tell him that the casual Friday look was over—or had never been this casual.

Again, he was wearing faded jeans and a t-shirt, with a baggy checked shirt that had never been in style. And as much as Paige appreciated the worn jeans, they made him look like an indigent teenager. All he needed was the skateboard. And he was the head of a company staffed by supermodels?

Even though Paige's brain registered the guy's poor choice of clothing, the rest of her didn't seem to care. And there were plenty of smaller, more eclectic restaurants without dress codes that she would love to try.

When they walked out of the building into the warmth of a late sunny afternoon, Paige tried to think of where they could go that was within walking distance. But Siegfried was moving ahead, so she hurried after him, figuring that he was more familiar with the neighborhood.

Paige followed even as he crossed against the traffic. Either Siegfried didn't notice the vehicles or he thought himself invincible, but Paige was not so confident. By the time she reached the opposite sidewalk, she felt lucky to be alive, and it took her a moment to realize that her companion had disappeared into a group of sightseers.

Paige stood there blinking at the mass of people, trying not to feel like a panicked mother who had lost her child. After all, Siegfried was an adult who could fully function on his own. Right? Paige wasn't so sure.

So when the crowd shifted to reveal him, she felt a surge of relief. However, it dissipated as she realized he was standing in front of some kind of vending booth for tourists, taking possession of two hot dogs.

He turned around, looking a bit perplexed, until his gaze lighted on her. When his expression cleared, it was so endearing that Paige walked toward him, even though she had the sinking feeling he was going to ask her if she wanted mustard. But no. Surely, even Siegfried wouldn't order up junk food off the street without even consulting her?

She told herself that he wouldn't, but soon her worst fears—and more—were confirmed. As Paige watched in disbelief, he looked at her guilelessly, hot dogs in hand. Then he asked her the question no woman wants to hear, especially from a male at mealtime.

"Do you have any money?"

CHAPTER EIGHT

Too late, Paige remembered Mia's claim that Siegfried didn't carry cash. And, of course, no driver or flunky was around to handle it for him. There was only Paige, forced to pick up the tab for her business lunch with a billionaire. Such was the wacky world of the Maitlands.

Paige swallowed a sigh at the lunch that might have been, but it was difficult to get too annoyed amid the sunshine and ambience of The Embarcadero. The palm-tree-lined boulevard along the waterfront was a beautiful area, and Paige realized it had been awhile since she'd been here—or taken a minute away from work.

This *was* work, Paige reminded herself. But it was easy to forget that in such surroundings. There were plenty of open spaces among the office buildings, and Siegfried soon found an unoccupied bench.

As Paige took a seat beside him, he hesitated, and she wondered whether he planned to share with her or if she was to forage for her own food. But then he turned and handed her the sandwich, his eyes focusing so intently on her that Paige was the one who faltered.

"You aren't a vegetarian, are you?" he asked, his brows lifting slightly under an unruly lock of hair.

Paige shook her head, although vegetarians wouldn't be the only ones who would refuse this meal. She really ought to take over his diet. Maybe Bebe could get someone to put a plate of veggies by his computer or have the cook mix up some protein shakes. There ought to be some way to get him to eat regularly, Paige mused, only to conjure a vision of shared candlelight dinners.

She promptly choked.

Siegfried slapped her on the back so hard that Paige coughed and held up a hand to stop him. Maybe this wasn't such a great idea. Straightening, she cleared her throat and her mind. It was time to get back to business.

"About the wedding," Paige said, grabbing her phone. "We have a date that your grandmother assures me is fine." She held the screen up for his approval, but he seemed more interested in the gadget itself than the data.

When he got an intent look on his face, she snatched back her device, just in case he decided to fool with the apps or, worse yet, take it apart.

"That date will be all right, then? It's convenient for you, too?" Paige asked. She tried not to remember that this was the kind of guy who had to be locked up in his own office to keep an appointment.

He nodded absently, so Paige continued. "The ceremony and reception will be held at your family's estate. I'll get some staff in to spruce up the gardens. In addition to the temporary help, your grandmother has asked me to hire some permanent employees."

Paige paused, but he said nothing, so she assumed tacit agreement. "Of course, we'll put up some tents. Evening. Dinner. Formal," she said, ticking off her notes. He didn't have to be involved in the menu or anything, did he? Just how detailed a report was she supposed to give him?

Paige glanced up to gauge his reaction and found those big brown eyes on her with an intensity that made her pause. For a moment, she had the giddy sensation that he was as interested in her as he'd been in the workings of her phone, and it didn't feel one bit businesslike.

The breath left her lungs in a rush, while his dark gaze seemed to draw her in closer and closer. It was only when Paige caught herself leaning toward him that she remembered this was not a date.

This was a professional meeting involving the most important wedding of her career, for which this guy just happened to be footing the bill. And she could not afford to jeopardize it. Straightening abruptly, Paige pasted on a smile.

"Is that all satisfactory?" she asked. "Your grandmother

seemed to feel that you must approve everything."

Instead of answering, Siegfried continued studying her until Paige felt herself flushing. "Do you do this a lot? Plan other people's weddings?" he asked.

The question was kind of insulting, but then again, how often did Siegfried get out of his lab or his office prison? "Yes. It's my business," Paige said.

"How did you get into it? Did you go to school for it?"

"Uh, no. They don't have a degree in wedding planning yet, as far as I know. I didn't have anything particular in mind when I majored in business at community college."

Paige had only known that she didn't want to end up like her mother, working unskilled jobs for low pay. She yearned for security and a better life, far away from where she grew up.

"I just sort of fell into the wedding thing. I had a friend who wanted me to plan hers, and it went from there. Word of mouth really," Paige said.

By the time she graduated, she had her business. She could have stayed in Indiana and built on that small base, but she had bigger ideas. "So I decided to try it full time and moved here."

"Why San Francisco?" Siegfried asked.

Paige took a deep breath. Normally, she refused to get into personal conversations with clients. She did her job, and that was enough, but there was too much riding on this account to brush him off.

So Paige found herself telling him far more than her usual brief bio, like why she loved the city she had adopted, how much she enjoyed pulling off an efficient, well-put-together show, and what Zoe contributed to her success.

"She attended one of my weddings, came up afterward with congratulations and suggestions, and we've been together ever since," Paige explained. She believed in hard work to get ahead, but there was still an element of luck, such as meeting Zoe—and Bebe.

"But you do all the organizing," Siegfried said, his gaze still intent upon her.

"Well, yes. I enjoy it," Paige said. Some people thought she liked to manage everything *too* well, but as she often told Zoe, at least she was using her control freak tendencies for good, not evil.

"We need someone like you," Siegfried said, so earnestly that Paige felt a traitorous leap of delight—until she realized he was referring to her work. Duh.

"Thank you. I hope to give you the wedding of the year," Paige said, looking down at her phone.

"I'm not talking about that," he said.

"Oh. But I'm afraid I wouldn't meet the criteria for employment at The Maitland Company," Paige said lightly, although the admission was grating. "It appears that all the job candidates must be tall, thin, and abnormally beautiful."

When Siegfried eyed her blankly, Paige lifted a brow. Even the boy genius couldn't be that blind to the supermodels who surrounded him.

"You're telling me that you haven't noticed your building is staffed by women who could walk the runways?" she asked.

Siegfried looked puzzled, as though trying to remember what his own assistant looked like. Maybe he was gay, Paige thought, fighting down a surge of disappointment.

"I mostly work with the tech people and my research team," he said with a hapless shrug.

Maybe he really hadn't noticed. Or maybe he didn't see the office help because he came to work through a secret tunnel or by heliport, Paige thought. Anything seemed possible as far as the Maitlands were concerned. But then who hired all the hotties?

"Who's Blake?" Paige asked.

"He's my cousin," Siegfried said, his warm voice suddenly flat. "He runs the sales end of the company."

So maybe it was Blake who did the hiring, while Siegfried was oblivious but, hopefully, not *too* oblivious.

"What, exactly, do you do?" Paige asked.

Siegfried looked so surprised, Paige wondered if she'd made some kind of faux pas. Was his work common knowledge, or was it top secret?

She figured the latter was more likely, considering the level of security. But he answered her readily enough. "Right now I'm focusing on robotics."

"Really? That's what Tad was so concerned about?" Paige asked, dumbfounded. To her, the word conjured up bad sci-fi movies or metal dogs that mimicked real pets, not exactly the kind of thing that required armed guards.

But Siegfried nodded. "It's a very competitive field, whether you're talking machines for production, in factories and labs, or for home use, which is what I'm working on. Everyone's looking for the killer app."

Paige blinked.

"The software that will take everything to the next level," Siegfried explained.

But Paige was still stuck on the "for home use" comment. "You're telling me you're making something like C3PO?"

Siegfried looked a bit blank, and Paige wondered if the guy had ever seen a movie. "A life-sized metal man who walks and talks?"

Siegfried shook his head. "Artificial intelligence is not limited to the humanoid model, though people do respond more positively to it. Right now, we are focusing on specific tasks, expanding the capabilities of machines already used for sorting and lifting packages, household chores, home health care, aiding disabilities, that type of work."

"Really? I didn't realize robots were used so much."

"Oh yeah. There are robots that can play and improvise music, flip pancakes, dispense medicine, step in for police, teach autistic children." He launched into a long explanation of the various types of machines available, who was using them, for what purpose, and what the future promised.

Sometimes he lapsed into techno-speak, but when he did, Paige just focused on the way he spoke and how good he looked when he did. She would never have dreamed that the guy could be so articulate.

"We're adding sensory capabilities and costs are coming

down, so it's really the beginning of the robotic revolution," he said, in all seriousness.

Imagining some sci-fi takeover, Paige lifted a brow.

"Just like the industrial revolution, only this time robots will be taking over most of today's jobs," he explained.

"Hopefully not that of wedding planner," Paige said with a smile.

Siegfried paused to look into her eyes. "Hopefully not," he said in a near whisper.

Something in the way his voice dipped made Paige forget all about occupations and focus on his mouth. Catching herself, she looked away, only to notice how late it was getting. The day was growing cooler, and the buildings were emptying their occupants.

Paige felt a sense of alarm. How long had they been sitting here? They had finished discussing the wedding awhile ago, moving on to personal information that had nothing to do with the upcoming event.

As the professional, Paige had only herself to blame for the lapse. Surging to her feet, she put her phone in her bag and hurried to make her excuses.

"I'm sorry. I didn't realize I was taking up so much of your time."

Siegfried gazed up at her with an expression of puzzlement. Was he as surprised as she was by the hour? Keeping to a schedule was not his strong suit. Did he even know where he was supposed to be now?

"Are they expecting you back in the office?" Paige asked.

He still looked confused, so Paige gestured toward the nearby building that housed The Maitland Company. "Do you have a lab there, too?"

"What? Oh, yeah. State of the art. But I prefer my grandfather's—the one at home," he said. Suddenly, his expression cleared. "I suppose I ought to get back there." Rising to his feet, he gazed at her expectantly.

What did he want, to shake on the deal? "Well, it's been

very nice doing business with you," Paige said, holding out her hand.

But instead of shaking it, Siegfried took it in both of his. Warm and rough-textured, they held hers in a loose grasp that stole her breath. She glanced at him in startlement, her heart pounding at the unexpected contact.

"Can you give me a ride?" he asked.

Paige returned to earth with a thud. Didn't the guy have a driver, or drivers, with a fleet of luxury vehicles at his beck and call? She felt like asking him if they were all out of service, but realized she couldn't be that rude, especially to such an important client.

"Of course," she said instead. But as soon as the words left her mouth, Paige regretted them. Now she had the drive out to the estate ahead of her. Again. With Siegfried. In what was rapidly becoming a reflex, Paige told herself that the wedding of the year would be worth the effort.

It was all for her business.

CHAPTER NINE

As the gates of the Maitland estate came into view, twin lampposts shining like beacons in the twilight, Paige felt a curious tingle of warmth. It was almost like coming home, whisking through the security and taking that long, curving driveway to the top of the cliffs.

She drew in a sharp breath as she realized the place was becoming way too familiar. But wasn't familiarity supposed to breed contempt?

And just this morning, hadn't she sworn not to accept another invitation here? Yet, when Siegfried wouldn't allow her to play the chauffeur and drop him off, she let him direct her toward the garages. And when he insisted she go in, she agreed, if only for a moment.

But once Bebe caught sight of them, there was no easy exit. The older woman was sure that Paige had brought Siegfried home to dinner, and none of Paige's protests changed her mind.

Not wanting to displease her client, Paige lingered. If she left, Siegfried might head for his secret lab, disappointing his grandmother and forgetting to eat. After all, the guy couldn't survive on one hot dog.

So Paige found herself once more at the Maitland table, which didn't seem quite as weird the second time around. Or maybe she was just becoming inured to it all? At least the tattooed and pierced Lila was back, which made for much less confusion, and the meal proceeded without any mishaps.

The group was also smaller and not quite as vocal as the other night. Uncle Otto was there, welcoming Paige like a, well, Dutch uncle, and she was surprised by her own pleasure at seeing him again. Lorenzo, too, was effusive in his greeting, while Linde was more reserved. But then there was Mia Anderson, smirking as usual, an addition Paige could have done without.

But with fewer at the table, the room wasn't quite as chaotic. It seemed less like a set piece from a movie and more like a real place where people congregated for good food and wine and conversation. And this time she was able to sit by Siegfried, rather than strangers, though the boy genius certainly wasn't the most vocal of partners.

Unfortunately, that designation went to Mia Anderson, who didn't seem to ingest anything, yet talked incessantly—sniping, dissing, and generally acting the spoiled heiress. Maybe she was eager for fresh blood, or she had a grudge against wedding planners since she was unmarried. Whatever the reason, Mia seemed to enjoy sharpening her talons on Paige, who could only bite her tongue since Mia was a member of the family that had retained her services.

"So your job is to fold other peoples' napkins?" Mia asked in a silky tone.

"No. That's the responsibility of the catering staff," Paige answered.

"Do you make the little favors then? Bags of dried flowers or something?"

"Uh, no."

"Paige will be organizing everything and making sure each person appears promptly," Bebe said.

Mia laughed. "Oh, that ought to be good. Are you going to lead Siegfried around on a leash or what?"

Paige bristled. Although Mia was a relative, this was still Siegfried's house. She glanced at him to gauge his reaction, but he seemed oblivious. In fact, he appeared to have tuned everyone out. He had laid down his fork and was staring off into space as though in the genius zone.

Paige wondered if she ought to hand-feed him, but her ensuing blush made her think better of that idea. She was not the guy's keeper, after all. So what business was it of hers if he starved to death? Or refused to look at her?

By the time dessert arrived, Paige was more than ready to get away from the entire Maitland clan, so she had her answer prepared when Bebe suggested she spend the evening.

"No, thank you. It was a wonderful meal, but I really must be going," Paige said.

"Oh, must you?" Bebe asked. The woman sounded so genuinely dismayed that Paige hesitated. But sincerity was all part of the Lady Bountiful persona, doubtlessly honed through years of charitable giving and politesse, so Paige could not take her protest personally. Nor was there any reason for her to stay.

The boy genius was still slumped in silence, probably lost in daydreams of circuitry, and whenever someone else tried to talk to Paige, Mia cut in. Paige was so tired of the jibes that one more might make her leap across the table and tear out the heiress's hair extensions. Or maybe even her hair. Which couldn't be good for business.

Paige stood.

"Well, I suppose we can't impose ourselves upon you any longer. But before you go, could you please show Siegfried your plans for the gardens?" Bebe asked, waving vaguely in the direction of the rear of the house.

Paige slanted a glance toward the end of the table, where a dark head was slumped over the tablecloth. At first, she thought he'd fallen asleep, but then she saw his hand moving. Was he writing on the tablecloth?

"Siegfried," she said. It was probably antique Belgian linen or something. Why, the size alone would make it worth a fortune.

He jerked up his head to stare at her, and the moment those brown eyes met her own, Paige felt the familiar loss of her breath. It was like being honed into focus by a pair of laser beams, so warm and intent that she felt giddy. And witless. What had she been planning to say?

Thankfully, she was saved by Bebe, who must have noticed her grandson's doodling, too. "Siegfried, you were writing on the tablecloth again," she said.

He looked down in surprise, as though astonished to discover material beneath his pen. Suddenly, Paige felt guilty for drawing attention to his behavior. "I have a piece of paper," she said, reaching for her bag.

"Of course you do," Mia said. Her sulky tone seemed to suggest that carrying writing materials was a sign of the lower classes. *Well, some of us work for a living*, Paige thought.

Siegfried dutifully copied his scratching onto the paper Paige gave him. She was standing so close that it seemed natural to lay a hand on his broad back. Or smooth the dark hair that fell over his collar. But she didn't.

Flushing, she looked away only to come face-to-face with Mia's smirk. She could only hope the heiress hadn't gauged her intentions.

Apparently, Mia wasn't that perceptive. "Isn't paper a bit low-tech in this day and age?" she asked.

"I keep all business notes on my phone," Paige said stiffly.

"Oh, Siegfried's had plenty of those, top of the line, experimental models," Mia said. "But he lost so many of them that he's not allowed to have any more."

Paige bristled. She hated the way Siegfried's family talked about the guy as though he were mentally challenged or incapable of handling his own affairs. He was a grown man, a brilliant scientist who was running a company and providing for everyone here. She bit her tongue to keep silent, but her expression must have given her away.

"Well, really, Mia," Bebe scolded. She turned toward Paige and lowered her voice. "It's because of security, you see."

"What?" Paige asked.

"Security. Can't have our boy's work lying around for just anyone to find," Mia said.

"Oh." Paige let out a low breath as she pictured Tad from the lab having a heart attack over that.

"There are people who would pay lots of money to get a copy of the genius's scribbles," Mia said. She looked directly at Paige when she spoke, as though casually tossing off an accusation of corporate espionage as a parting gift.

Paige lifted a brow at the not-so-subtle insinuation. The

thought of the airhead heiress being concerned about anything other than racking up charge cards and cavorting with the equally shallow was ludicrous.

When Paige didn't react, Mia's eyes narrowed. "But that kind of thing can be very dangerous," she warned.

"I hardly think anyone here is going to make off with the tablecloth," Bebe said. "Perhaps it will wash out."

"Not if he's using permanent ink, like he usually does," Mia argued.

But Bebe didn't seem concerned. "I'm sure Lila can take care of it. But don't lose your paper, Siegfried," she said. "And come along. Paige wants to show you where we'll be having the wedding."

Paige wondered about that subtle twisting of the facts. Wasn't it Bebe who had requested the tour? But she remained silent, while Siegfried stood up so fast he nearly knocked over his chair.

Paige tried not to look. Anywhere. Because if Mia was smirking, Paige wouldn't be responsible for her actions. The guy roused all of her protective instincts, she realized, which was kind of alarming. But it was nothing more than she might feel for a lost puppy, Paige assured herself.

By the time they reached the terrace, both Mia and Bebe had disappeared. While Paige was glad to see the last of the heiress, she wasn't comfortable being alone with Siegfried. Again. Thankfully, she had only to point out his own backyard to him before heading home.

But once she stepped outside, Paige's eagerness to leave evaporated into the night air. Surely, no one could be unaffected by such a setting. Quiet enveloped her, providing a welcome respite from the noisy dining room.

Stars twinkled overhead, while the scent of flowers and ocean wafted toward her on a gentle breeze. For a moment, it seemed like paradise there in the darkness, and Paige felt some sort of strange longing well up inside.

Beside her, Siegfried stirred and pointed upward. "Look,

there's a bolide."

"A what?" Paige said, her voice oddly shaky.

"Didn't you hear it? It's a fireball, a type of meteor that produces a sound like thunder."

"A meteor? You mean a shooting star," Paige said, as she saw a streak in the night sky. She resisted an urge to lean into the tall hunk of male, warm and appealing, who stood so near. Wasn't she supposed to be pointing things out to him, not vice versa? *Pay attention to business,* she told herself.

The reminder made her dismiss any romantic fantasies and see the venue for what it was, dark and overgrown, a veritable minefield for potential wedding guests. There were some older light fixtures by the patio, but their glow didn't begin to reach into the gardens.

"We'll need some better lighting out here," she said. She would have to get someone in to install permanent additions of which Bebe would approve. It had to be something classy but romantic, providing enough illumination so people could move about freely, yet still dance in the shadows.

Paige caught herself drifting into Zoe's territory and frowned. Her forte was the planning and organization, not the fairy dust. She stepped off the terrace, away from Siegfried, and immediately began to think more clearly.

"I see the tent being set up there," she said over her shoulder. "Of course, we'll have to clear some of the undergrowth, but it would be the perfect placement, close to the house, yet in the gardens and with a view of the ocean."

When nothing except silence met her words, Paige cleared her throat. But her businesslike manner faltered as she sensed Siegfried behind her. Had he moved closer?

The hairs on the back of her neck were standing up, as if in anticipation. But for all she knew he could have wandered off, struck by some sudden inspiration that did not involve her. Skateboards. Robots. Tablecloths.

She turned around, ready to call him to attention, only to bump into his tall form. He *was* closer. "Oh, sorry," she stammered, suddenly nervous. It was really dark away from the house. Maybe they should try this in the morning.

Siegfried reached out to steady her, his big hands gentle on her arms, and Paige's heart raced. She told herself that the guy was a client, a gawky genius with his head in another world far from her own.

But the warmth and scent of him drew her like some kind of magnet. In the darkness, he didn't seem awkward or clumsy or distracted, and his touch robbed her of her professionalism.

Why he should have this effect on her was a mystery. Obviously, she needed to get out more. Zoe was always trying to drag her to clubs and parties, but Paige was too busy, too focused on work to...

Before she could finish the thought, Siegfried leaned in and kissed her. Paige was so shocked that she nearly swallowed her tongue. Or was it his tongue?

For a boy genius who spent most of his time in a lab, he certainly seemed to know what to do with his mouth, and Paige couldn't help responding. Who wouldn't? She couldn't remember the last time she'd been kissed like this. Uh, maybe... never?

He slipped his arms around her, and Paige came up against his hard body. He might be slender, but what there was of him was firm. If this was what the skateboarding did for him, then she was all for it, she decided, latching onto him. And for once, she let herself feel absolute, delicious, abandon.

Until light flooded them.

"Well, well. Now whose wedding are we planning?"

The sound of Mia's voice, rife with scorn, roused Paige in a way that the sudden brightness had not. She pulled from Siegfried, startled to see that the terrace had additional lights that had not been turned on before. Harsh and bright, they were intended for security rather than ambience. Perhaps Tad had installed them.

Stepping backward, Paige blinked at Siegfried, who wore a slumberous expression that made her want to move right back into his arms. She had the distinct feeling that if she let him, he'd lead her up to his bedroom or even into the bushes, no matter how awkward he might appear sometimes.

But the sight of Mia, lounging against the doors, smoking a cigarette, put those thoughts to flight.

"Well, well, it looks like a lawsuit's not the only way to get some Maitland money," she said in a mocking tone.

Her comment made Paige suck in a breath. She was not here to squeeze Siegfried for cash or anything else, but she wasn't about to get into it with the heiress.

"I have to be going," Paige said. "If you'll excuse me." She nodded stiffly at Siegfried. Although he gave her a puzzled look, he didn't try to stop her as she brushed past him, a lack of action that said everything Paige needed to know. Or so she told herself.

As she headed across the patio, Paige met Mia's sneer with a challenging stare, having had enough of the girl's taunting. But she was angriest with herself for getting into such an awkward position.

She was a businesswoman, and the way to reach the top in her profession was not to sleep with a client. Or the brother of a client. Or the head of the family. It was like sleeping with the father of the bride.

And Paige was not a romantic. It was her job to set up the kind of atmosphere that had nearly seduced her: the starry night, the ocean breeze, and the perfume of flowers all combining to create some magical place that existed only in fantasies. Reality, as she well knew, was something else entirely.

Once inside the house, Paige avoided everyone by making her way out through the garages. But it wasn't until she passed through the gates that she let out a long breath of relief. She had escaped both the wacky family and what could have turned into a bad situation.

So why didn't she feel better?

Paige swallowed hard as she headed down the hill in the darkness, alone, on the way to her tiny apartment and the work that surely had accumulated in her absence. She was better off at home, away from the rambling Maitland estate with its crazy characters and temptations out of another world.

She had worked hard to get where she was, Paige told herself as she opened the door of her spartan studio. And this was where she belonged. With a glance around at the familiar walls, she settled in for the night and tried not to think about what she had left behind.

CHAPTER TEN

Siegfried stood staring after Paige as she hurried back into the house. What had happened? One minute she was all soft and delicious and the next she was stiff and angry. Although he could master the complexities of AI programming, the reactions of real people were beyond him.

Should he go after her? He didn't want her to leave, but she seemed pretty determined to get out of here. Maybe he should just call her name? But if she stopped, what would he say? As usual, the social niceties escaped him.

How did anyone do this? Maybe he ought to start watching television or movies to get a clue. But whenever he tried, he usually got interested in something else and the stuff on the screen went on without him.

As he waited, undecided, Mia pushed away from the door. "What was that about?"

Siegfried knew her act well. A mass of insecurities, she lashed out so that people wouldn't notice. But tonight he just didn't feel like dealing with her.

It was bad enough that she had ruined the first kiss he'd had in... He couldn't even remember. He wasn't going to listen to her mock him for it. Ducking his head, he strode toward the house.

"Well, well," she said as he passed her. "I didn't think you had it in you. And all this time, we thought you were gay."

Siegfried refused to take the bait. She certainly had more experience with the opposite sex than he did, but not one lasting relationship to her credit. And knowing Mia, if he asked for her help, she would delight both in tormenting him and giving him the wrong advice.

So he said nothing and focused on the sequence of events. Everything had seemed to go well until dinner. That's when he had lost control of the experiment, er, situation. It was his own fault, of course. He had little use for others and often tuned them out, his cousin especially.

When Mia opened her mouth, his shut. One moment he would be watching her talk, and the next he would be struck with a great idea for simulating human movement in robots. Maybe it was because Mia acted so much like an AI, without the I.

Tonight had been no different. The regular conversation that went round the table had turned into a buzzing in his ears, and then he had a sudden idea that had taken his attention away from it all, including Paige. He drew in a long breath.

When he was alone with her, nothing distracted him. On The Embarcadero, he had talked and watched and listened, his attention solely on her. She had this glow about her that he couldn't explain, like an aurora borealis that only he could see.

She used her hands while she spoke, graceful little movements that she didn't even realize she made, but that were fascinating to study. You couldn't program that kind of spontaneous stuff.

Of course, you couldn't replicate anything like Paige Porter, even with a 3D printer. When Willow told him she was coming to the office, Siegfried had made his assistant promise to lock him up, if necessary, to make sure he didn't miss her.

He was fully aware of his tendency to lose track of time and meetings. Lack of focus, his teachers had claimed, but usually it was too much focus on what interested him and too little patience for the rest.

Then it had been school that bored him, but now it was business. All the meetings began the same way, with some idiot, usually Blake, beginning a long speech on some boring topic to try to prove he was useful. And Siegfried was gone—if not physically, then mentally.

He hated the business stuff and preferred being left alone to work on his projects, like his father and grandfather before him. But, as head of the family, he was head of the company, so he was supposed to handle it.

All the demands left him with little time for anything else, but he had sworn he would make time for Paige. And he had.

Thankfully, Bebe had given him another chance after tonight's dinner by suggesting Paige show him her plans for the garden. And he had been aware enough to seize his opportunity. But then it had gone wrong.

Was she mad about the kiss? She seemed to be enjoying it at the time, but Siegfried had learned long ago that there were subtle nuances to behavior that he couldn't quite grasp. If only there were a tech manual for human interaction.

"Hello? What are you doing? I thought you were going to chase after your little businesswoman."

The sound of Mia's taunts made Siegfried swing round, and he realized that he had halted in the hall, lost in thought.

"Wait till Bebe finds out that you've scared off her prized planner," Mia said with a smirk. "Have you thought about that? What if she quits?"

Siegfried blinked at her, uncomprehending.

"Hello? Sexual harassment," she said. "And even if she doesn't slap you with a civil suit to divest you of the Maitland cash, she'll probably slam us, which means Bebe will have to look for a new napkin folder. And you know how hard it is to get anyone to work here."

Mia's complaints segued into her ongoing scheme to put the family in a reality television show, thereby giving herself even more exposure and pocketing some much-needed money. Since nobody else in the household would agree, she took every opportunity to pitch the program. But Siegfried was already tuning her out, although a couple of her comments lingered like a bad error message.

He hadn't harassed Paige, had he? He was definitely out of the loop when it came to such things, but he couldn't imagine a kiss being illegal. Of course, it had been more than that. He couldn't remember ever feeling that good.

After the last time Blake had set him up with someone, Siegfried had crawled into his lab, giving up on sex completely. And he hadn't really missed it. Until now.

But Paige made him aware of what he had been doing without, or, more accurately, what he had been searching for, since his previous experiences in that area had left him wanting. The whole romance thing had eluded him all of his life until it seemed like some great metaphysical question waiting to be answered.

And like anything worth knowing, it wasn't going to be easy to discover. Already he had faced his first setback.

Although Siegfried never let anything stop him where his work was concerned, he didn't know whether he could apply that same determination to the human sphere, which was far more volatile and challenging than robotics. He was well aware of his own limitations, but he had a gut feeling that he should focus his energy on a new project.

Project Paige.

"You *what?*"

The sound of Zoe's shriek, raised to a deafening pitch, made Paige wince. She hadn't meant to mention the kiss or kisses or whatever. In fact, she had sworn to keep that detail to herself, but somehow during the course of Zoe's intense questioning as to why she hadn't been back to meet with the Maitlands in more than a week, Paige had caved.

Obviously, she wouldn't do well under torture.

Paige blamed the ice cream, which had lulled her into complacency. Now that a creamery had opened nearby, Zoe was always forcing her to hold "staff sessions" there for the two of them.

Paige couldn't imagine any other business people meeting in an ice cream shop, except perhaps the head of The Maitland Company. She smiled at the thought of Siegfried here. Sloppy. Enjoying himself. Licking his luscious lips.

"No!" Zoe said, snatching the bowl right out from under Paige's spoon. "Not one bite until you spill the whole story."

Paige couldn't begin to explain to her stomach why the world's most decadent ice cream, hand-mixed on a slab of frozen granite right in front of her eyes, was suddenly pulled away. So she caved. Again.

"He kissed me," Paige mumbled, snatching the bowl back.

"By he, you mean Siegfried Maitland, heir apparent of the Maitland family, CEO of The Maitland Company, and one of the Bay Area's most eligible bachelors?"

Paige shrugged and dipped her spoon into her mix before it could be taken from her again.

"So what then? Did you sleep with him? Did you sleep with Siegfried Maitland?" Zoe's question rang out loudly enough to make Paige choke. Shaking her head in a vicious negative, she kicked her assistant under the table.

"All right. All right. So you didn't sleep with him," Zoe said, lowering her voice. She paused to study Paige intently. "Why not?"

Paige nearly choked again. "Because he's a client," she whispered.

"Hello? He's not the one getting married, is he?"

Paige refused to be swayed by Zoe's weird brand of logic. "He's the one paying for it," she said. "He's the one leading the bride down the aisle." Or at least that's what Paige thought. They hadn't gotten that far yet.

Regardless, it wasn't right. "It's like sleeping with the bride's father," Paige said.

"Yeah, right." Zoe snorted. "And anyway, what's so wrong with that? As long as the guy doesn't currently have a wife." Her head tilting, she paused to consider her own question. "I suppose it would depend on just how old he was and how good-looking."

"And how rich," Paige added dryly.

Zoe laughed at the barb, but Paige glanced at her in sudden horror. "Please don't tell me you've slept with any of our clients, either the grooms or the fathers."

"Why shouldn't I, if I like the guy?" Zoe asked.

Paige groaned and snatched away her assistant's bowl.

"All right. All right," Zoe said, retrieving her concoction. "I haven't."

"And you won't?" Paige prompted.

"And I won't," Zoe said, making a face. Then she dove into her ice cream with obvious relish. There was nothing small about Zoe's tastes, and Paige had to smile at her expression of bliss.

The peace lasted about as long as it took Zoe to swallow. "But, anyway, that has nothing to do with Siegfried Maitland," she said. "He's not a client or the father of one."

Paige groaned again. Why couldn't Zoe just drop it? It was bad enough that she had thought of little else for the past week. She had been over and over the, uh, incident, in her mind, and she could only come to one conclusion: She couldn't risk the business.

After years of building her reputation, she finally had a chance at the elite customers. And she wasn't going to blow it because of a couple kisses, even if they were pretty extraordinary. Paige frowned at the word and accused herself of exaggerating. A week of thinking about little else had obviously colored her memory.

Paige cleared her throat."Aren't we supposed to be discussing work?"

"You're scared, that's all," Zoe said. She licked her spoon. "You're afraid of getting involved with anyone. I've known you for what? Nearly three years. And you've never been on more than a few dates."

Paige felt her face redden. "I have a business to build, which doesn't leave me a lot of extra time."

Zoe shook her head. "You make time for what's important."

Paige pushed at the ice cream in her bowl. It was easy for Zoe to talk. She had stocks and bonds from her mom and dad and a great little apartment in North Beach. Although a faithful employee, she looked on the job as more of a lark, a time-killer until she met her rich husband.

To Paige it was life itself. She was her own self support, and whatever she wanted she had to provide for herself with her profits. She lived frugally, but she didn't want to do so forever, and only a successful business would guarantee that she didn't have to, as well as getting her the one perk she most desired: a home of her own.

Paige's mom had done her best, but a series of rentals hadn't felt permanent, not like the places other kids had, with the requisite two parents, some siblings, and a backyard with a swing set.

Older and wiser now, Paige knew that no one had a perfect family, but she still longed for a house with some ground, a retreat that would be hers for as long as she wanted. It was silly, really, when a condo would be more practical, but she had her dream, and she had worked long and hard to get it, putting herself through college, starting out small, and growing when she could.

Since this was the Bay Area, one of the priciest spots for real estate in the world, her goal was taking longer to reach, but that only made it more worthwhile. After all her hard work, Paige wasn't about to put her dreams—her job—in jeopardy because of some good-looking guy, even if he was the best kisser ever. And it was just common sense to never mix business with pleasure, something Zoe, the more free-spirited of the two of them, didn't understand.

"When I've built up the business to the level I'd like, then I'll get around to all that stuff you keep bugging me about, like taking vacations and dating," Paige said.

"And just when will that be?" Zoe asked with a skeptical glance.

"I don't know. Maybe after the Maitland wedding," Paige said. But she knew that's when things would really start taking off and she would need to be around more than ever.

Zoe shook her head. "You are missing the opportunity of a lifetime."

"What? Just because he's rich?" Paige said, frowning.

"No. Because he's young and handsome and rich," Zoe said with a grin. "And because you like him. I can tell."

For some reason, Paige flushed again. "Right. I like him as well as any lost kid who needs looking after," she said. "I'm not cut out to be a nursemaid."

Zoe sighed over her empty bowl. "That's too bad because it certainly sounds like he needs someone."

At her words, Paige felt a sudden lurch in the region of her chest. She wished she could just laugh off Zoe's comment with a smart reply. After all, what could a young, handsome, rich genius, with gorgeous models staffing his company, possibly need? But all of her instincts told her Siegfried Maitland did need someone.

It just couldn't be her.

Siegfried leaned away from the computer screen with a sigh. A firm believer in research, he was determined to find some kind of advice online about Project Paige. But so far he had just found a lot of porn. A lot. Who knew there was that much out there?

He was glad he wasn't in the office, but in the lab under the house, so that no one could be shocked by some of the things that had popped up. Hell, he'd been shocked. But the only other soul here was Tad, standing sentinel in the corner. Did the guy never sit down?

Siegfried rubbed the back of his neck and frowned at the screen. Almost as numerous were the matchmaking sites. But he wasn't looking for a date. He'd found one. He just needed to know how to get her back—or maybe get her in the first place.

If only there were a book that could tell him. But it seemed that most of the relationship texts catered to women, with titles like *Get the Guy of Your Dreams*, *Why Men Love Bitches*, and *Don't Get Dumped!*

The men's references leaned more toward sex. Somehow Siegfried couldn't picture having *How to Get Laid* delivered to his office. And it wasn't what he was looking for anyway, unless there was a chapter on "How to Get Laid by Paige."

There were several books about how to succeed with women, plural, but they made him picture some loser trolling bars with his fly open. It was definitely not the image he was after.

When he finally did find some titles to order, he had them

sent to the house, where he wouldn't have to suffer Willow's pitying glances or take the chance that Blake might get wind of his purchases. He even had the sense to call upstairs and have Godfrey watch for the delivery.

Thankfully, the butler sent the package down unopened and without comment beyond a lift of his bushy eyebrows. And Siegfried grabbed the box before Tad could get a hold of it and check for bombs or hidden cameras.

Once back at the computer, Siegfried lifted out the first volume and rifled through it. *The Average Guy's Guide to Dating* listed some tricks, but he wasn't interested in pick-up lines or self-confidence boosters.

He glanced at the sections on manners and clothing and groaned. Was he supposed to wear a suit? How was that going to make Paige appear on his doorstep?

The book about opposing planets dating seemed promising, but there were no real analogies to the planets. He didn't get that. What was the point of the title?

And the advice to not be yourself threw him. Who was he supposed to be? His thoughts wandered to the androgynous properties of robot prototypes, and he tossed the book aside.

Leaning back in his chair, he put up a hand to rub his neck and saw Tad eyeing him with a frown. Hopefully, the security guard hadn't noticed his recent interest in porn, or he was sure to get a lecture on internet hazards... Unless Tad was looking at it, too, on one of his monitors.

The thought made Siegfried glance up again, and he studied the guard more intently. Tad was a guy, a few years older than he, who must have a life outside of his job. Siegfried couldn't remember the man ever talking about that life, but they didn't have a lot of casual conversations.

"So, Tad," Siegfried said. "Are you, uh, dating anyone?"

For once, the stone-faced guard reacted, his lips tightening into a thin line that looked awfully like disapproval. Siegfried had screwed up again. He hoped the guard didn't think he was coming on to him and hurried to correct any misconception.

"Uh, I was just wondering because I met this girl, and I'm

not, uh, sure how to proceed," Siegfried muttered.

Tad did not appear relieved by the explanation. In fact, his expression grew even fiercer. "I really would advise against any relationships with strange women, sir."

What? Was he gay, or was he warning against strangers of either sex? Or prostitutes? "She's not a stranger," Siegfried said.

"I just mean that any kind of personal intimacy with someone outside of your immediate circle poses security risks, for you, your family, and The Maitland Company," Tad said soberly.

So his only option was incest? Siegfried shuddered at the thought of Mia, whose exploits were probably amongst those that had popped up on his screen earlier.

"Tad, all of us have contact with other people," Siegfried said. But then he wondered just how long it had been since he'd met someone outside of the company, except for a few of the people Bebe befriended, most of whom were far older than he.

"Yes, but the other family members aren't privy to the sort of highly classified information that you are," Tad said.

What? So he wasn't allowed to meet anyone for fear he would suddenly come up with the killer app and blurt it out to whoever was sitting next to him? Or did Tad think he was going to talk about the work in his sleep to his bedmate—if he ever got anyone into bed, which was highly doubtful at this point?

No wonder he was trapped in the lab all the time like some kind of research animal, Siegfried thought, with a trace of resentment. "Did Blake put you up to this?" he asked, studying the security guard with new suspicion.

"Up to what, sir?" Tad asked, his face expressionless.

"To keeping me from the world," Siegfried said, bitterness creeping into his tone.

"I thought you preferred the facility to outside activities," Tad said. Siegfried frowned. Up until a few days ago he had, eschewing the mindless chatter of the usual idiots for the stimulation of his own thoughts. But that was B.P.—Before Paige.

"Well, I can't stay in here all the time," Siegfried said, suddenly regretting his own habits. "No matter what Blake wants."

"Mr. Blake Maitland might have hired me, sir, but I am loyal to everyone in this family," Tad said stiffly.

"Of course," Siegfried muttered, annoyed at having voiced his thoughts aloud. Again, his lack of social skills was showing. Not only was he still without any advice, but he had insulted Tad. Maybe he should avoid all human interaction.

But then he would have to give up on Project Paige, which he wasn't ready to do. Tossing aside one of the useless books, Siegfried was wondering where else to look for help when he realized that he could go up to dinner.

Normally, he didn't pay much attention to meals, but now there was the possibility that she might be there, so he stood up and ran a hand through his messy hair. Wasn't he supposed to get it cut soon?

Maybe it would help to look a bit better. He glanced down at his worn jeans and decided there was no way he was going to put on a suit. Did he even own one that fit? Shaking his head, he hurried toward the elevator before he got distracted by anything else.

He still had no strategy, no plan, no real hope, but sometimes, even in science, you had to go with your hunches.

CHAPTER ELEVEN

Sometimes hunches were wrong.

When Siegfried got to the dining room, there were a lot of people at the table, but none of them were Paige, and he felt an almost painful disappointment at the discovery. He ate without tasting anything, his usual disinterest in food even more pronounced.

For once, he wasn't preoccupied with thoughts of work, either, so he didn't bother to get out his pen. Instead, he mulled over the Paige problem, as attached to it as he had once been to a programming paradigm.

"You are not looking so well tonight, Siegfried, my boy."

Siegfried glanced up from his plate to find Uncle Otto studying him benignly.

"In fact, you look as though you've lost your best friend," the older man said.

Siegfried frowned. He didn't have a best friend. If he did, he could ask the bro what to do about Paige. Although he sometimes hung out with the tech guys on his teams, he doubted they could give him any advice. Most of them were so into work that their social lives were limited to conferences and demonstrations of new devices.

"Are you having a problem with your robots?" Otto asked.

Siegfried shook his head.

"Sometimes it helps to talk about the difficulties."

Siegfried shook his head again. "It's not work," he muttered.

"Ah! So it is a girl, yes?" Otto said, with a knowing nod.

Siegfried didn't answer. For no apparent reason, he felt himself flushing. Paige was no girl, but a woman, with all the right curves. He ought to know. He had felt them pressed against him. The memory of that night in the garden came rushing back, and he closed his eyes, trying to recapture it like a lost equation.

By the time he opened them again, the news, or rather the misconception that he had female problems, had spread like a bad virus. Everyone around him was buzzing with it.

"Siegfried has a girl?" An older woman farther down the table screeched the question loudly, and he shuddered.

Suddenly, after the dearth of advice, he was getting way too much of it—simultaneously—as everyone urged him to pursue "the girl" and asked about her. The only one who wasn't talking was Mia, which was never a good sign.

The smirk on her face confirmed his suspicions. Whatever else anyone might try to do to help him, Mia would work just as hard to destroy whatever chances he might have. And even Siegfried could tell that any advice offered by those at the Maitland table would be well-intentioned but worthless.

With a sinking feeling, he suspected he might as well give up now instead of wasting his time. A smart researcher knew when to abandon an experiment that wasn't working, that had no hope of success. Cut your losses early on, he remembered one professor telling him.

It wasn't something Siegfried liked hearing—or doing—especially when he had invested heavily in a project. And he wasn't thinking about money, but time, energy, and, in this case, emotion. Groaning, he lurched to his feet, mumbled some excuse, and fled back to the familiar isolation of his lab, where at least he could control the variables.

He hoped that his quick exit from the dinner table would put an end to all speculation about him. After all, he wasn't around people much, even those who lived in his own house. But he had forgotten how quickly news traveled through the Maitland estate.

He was reminded soon enough.

It started the very next morning when he got into the car to head to the office. Arthur, his burly driver, rolled down the partition to eye him in the mirror.

"You got lady problems, Mr. Siegfried?" he asked, his New York accent still intact. "Give 'em flowers. That's what I do.

Young or old, the ladies like their flowers."

Siegfried could only nod painfully before putting the glass between them. But when the receptionist on his floor winked at him, he knew he was in trouble—and probably the butt of every joke throughout the building. He only hoped that Blake hadn't heard.

Siegfried had barely recovered from Blake's last stunt. When Siegfried had naively agreed to his cousin's offer to hook him up, he had been stuck with a high-priced call girl who demanded payment even though he couldn't perform. That had effectively ended all personal intercourse, so to speak, with his cousin.

Flushing at the memory, Siegfried veered away from his office and made his way down to the labs, where the tech guys could be counted on to care nothing about real life, his own or anyone else's.

And before long he was too caught up in his work to worry about what people were saying about him. But when someone mentioned breaking for dinner, Siegfried didn't ignore the suggestion, as he usually did, or let the others order in. Instead, he surged to his feet, paying no attention to their startled looks, and headed home, *just in case.*

Once there, he was reluctant to check out the occupants of the dining room because if Bebe saw him, he'd be trapped. And the thought of another evening spent surrounded by people discussing his nonexistent girlfriend was too much.

So he hung back in the hallway until he could catch someone. Luckily, Godfrey soon appeared, and Siegfried flagged him down.

"Is she here?" he asked, motioning the butler into an alcove.

"She is not," Godfrey said in his usual stiff-necked manner. One had to appreciate a butler who acted like talking to his employers was a painful chore. "And you call yourself a genius."

Siegfried blinked at the accusation. "I think that's an appellation others have stuck on me, especially my optimistic parents."

"And every tutor you ever had," Godfrey said.

Siegfried shrugged. He was used to not living up to expectations. Oh, he had come up with some useful patents, but nothing to equal his father and grandfather. And look how long he had been involved in robotics—long enough to come up with the killer app, as Blake kept reminding him.

Siegfried frowned. Suddenly, the life that had been so reliable and familiar, if not totally fulfilling, seemed stifling and annoying. "Well, I guess that just proves how wrong people can be," he muttered.

"But it doesn't explain your current inability to solve one simple problem," Godfrey said.

"What?" Siegfried said. His work might have stalled, but it was hardly simple.

The butler lifted his bushy eyebrows, an expression of haughty superiority on his face. "If you want to see her, simply go to one of her weddings."

"One of her weddings?" Siegfried echoed. The butler had lost him.

"She's a wedding planner," Godfrey said slowly. "That is her job. She must have weddings that she will oversee between now and your sister's."

The insight hit Siegfried with the force of a blow. It was such an easy answer, and yet he, with all his degrees, would never have thought of it.

"Great idea, Godfrey!" Siegfried said. Then he paused at the logistics. "But how?"

Godfrey gave him a look. "Have Willow make a few inquiries and get yourself invited to one of them. Or you could simply appear at the function."

"You mean crash someone's wedding?"

"Of course, I'm no genius, but I suspect that no one in the Bay Area is going to turn away a Maitland from any event," Godfrey said.

Siegfried frowned at the idea of trading on his birthright. He despised the fake friendliness of those who sought to use him for his money or his brains or his family's connections.

"Are you still there, sir?" Godfrey asked in his typically dry way.

Siegfried nodded.

"Good. Then there is one other thing," Godfrey said, eyeing him up and down with distaste. "Unless the couple are saying their vows in an abandoned parking lot, I suggest you have Willow dress you, as well."

At Siegfried's blank look, the butler sighed. "Have her send over someone from Armani, with a suit or a tux, whatever is suitable. Or I fear Ms. Porter will have you ejected from any proper gathering."

Siegfried glanced down at his faded jeans and t-shirt. Perhaps the man was right. "Thank you, Godfrey."

"You are entirely welcome," the butler said. Bowing slightly, he turned away, leaving Siegfried to get to a phone and call Willow before he forgot.

Paige stood at the sanctuary door, looking down the length of the room toward the altar and the transept where the organist played. Although she couldn't see the woman from where she was stationed, Paige knew Zoe was nearby, waiting for her next cue.

"Ready," Paige said into her headset.

A minute later the organist had finished playing. "Five. Four. Three. Two. One," Paige said.

"Go," Zoe answered, and the wedding march began.

This was a traditional ceremony, held in a church so large that just getting from one end to the other was a major expedition. But she and Zoe had the timing down to an art, and Paige smiled in satisfaction.

She enjoyed her work, and recently it held the added attraction of keeping her thoughts from drifting to a certain boy genius. But it was awfully hard to forget about the guy when she had been getting calls from people who lived in his house. She was beginning to wonder if she ought to put in a separate line to accommodate them.

Paige told herself that nothing about the Maitland household could surprise her, but this new development had been unusual, to say the least. Everyone who called had some suggestion for the wedding that they wanted her to run by Siegfried. Although Paige patiently told each person that they needed to direct any suggestions to Hilde, somehow she had become a sort of intermediary, presumably because Hilde never could be found.

In most cases, it was the bride who inundated her with calls, or sometimes the mother of the bride. This had to be the first time the bride's sister's vocal coach had gotten involved. Or someone like Uncle Otto.

He had been so insistent that she approach Siegfried with his suggestions that Paige had finally asked him why he couldn't talk to Siegfried himself, since they were living in the same house. Did the guy stay at the office or hide in his lab 24/7?

When Otto had offered no explanation, Paige found herself worrying about the Maitland heir. Where exactly was he, if unreachable? Was he eating? Was he sleeping? Did he have a cot in the basement, or did he simply collapse on a slab of metal like one of his robots? She pictured him red-eyed and wasting away, locked in his office or chained to a computer.

Paige shook her head. Why was she concerned about Siegfried Maitland? He was a big boy. A grown man. Tall. Strong... Paige drew in a sharp breath and focused on the ceremony in front of her.

The couple was returning, their faces beaming with that absurd glow newlyweds have, which lasted until after the honeymoon, maybe, if they were lucky. But hey, they looked great now, didn't they?

Paige turned on her heel to check the waiting cars, her thoughts already moving ahead to the dinner to follow. Thankfully, she would be too busy to dwell on the eating habits of the boy genius.

And as for all the suggestions she was supposed to discuss

with him, how about e-mail? She could get his address and never have to speak to him again. Right?

So why did the urge to meet with the guy in person keep nagging at her even while she oversaw the reception? Paige knew she wasn't concentrating when she became aware of the whispers around her, something she should have picked up on right away. Usually, she made it her business to know what was going on at all times.

Once in a while there were difficulties, with employees, with food, with music, or even with guests. A drunken relative could, intentionally or not, ruin the mood and bring the bride to tears.

On rare occasions, the troublemaker had to be escorted from the premises. More often they could be coaxed into better behavior with a bit of judicious handling.

So Paige always mingled on the edge of the gathering, keeping a sharp eye on everyone and everything. But tonight she was slow to pick up on the fact that someone was taking attention away from the bride, which was never a good thing.

She followed the direction of the looks. Heads were turning toward one of the guest tables. She didn't see or hear anything unusual coming from the area, but she moved in closer. There were several people sitting there, an older couple and two younger ones, all seemingly well behaved.

"I tell you, it's him. I can tell even from here." One of the nearby matrons was whispering loud enough for Paige to hear, and she discreetly cocked her head to listen.

"Nonsense. He never attends any public functions."

"Darling, it has to be him. He looks just like his father and his grandfather, too, for that matter."

"Didn't he blow himself up?"

"Yes. Some sort of lab accident. They're all mad as hatters."

"Or crazy like foxes. They're positively dripping money. Look at that mansion they have overlooking the bay."

"Prime real estate, but the house is positively ghastly," the other woman said. She turned toward the table that seemed to draw everyone's focus. "A teardown if there ever was one. But think of what you could do with the site."

She paused, her eyes narrowing in speculation. "My daughter Candy is divorced again. Wouldn't they make a lovely match?"

The first matron laughed. "Candy would eat him alive. Hasn't she already gone through two husbands?" The smile she gave her companion was a thinly veiled smirk. "Besides, I hear he's socially inept, a complete boor."

"Well, he looks presentable, and I'm sure he could be trained." The other woman, who had begun to resemble a viper, smiled evilly. "And with those billions, who cares?"

Paige stood still, listening longer than she might otherwise have done because of a growing sense of foreboding. She told herself that the two women could be talking about anyone, most likely some rich old geezer.

Just because Siegfried Maitland was perpetually on her mind did not mean he was the subject of their crude conversation. And yet, when Paige looked at the table under discussion, she noticed that one of the men had long dark hair that needed a good trim.

It couldn't be Siegfried because he never went anywhere. Right? And the cut of the clothes was too good. Paige had never seen him wear anything except his skateboarding outfit, even when in his office. He probably didn't even own a suit. Did he?

As though he could sense Paige's scrutiny, the man at the table slowly turned, and despite her suspicions, Paige gaped in shock. *What was Siegfried Maitland doing here?*

CHAPTER TWELVE

Paige hadn't seen any Maitlands on the guest list, and Siegfried never said anything to her about coming. But then why should he? And when? She hadn't talked to him since that night in the garden.

Paige flushed at the memory. *Let's not go there*, she told herself. But even as she tried to forget their last encounter, her gaze lingered on his familiar form, which looked incredible in a custom black suit.

No wonder every head in the place was turning toward him. He probably had half the men and every one of the women drooling over him, including her.

The thought drew Paige up short. She didn't know what he was up to, but it certainly wasn't her concern. With a perfunctory nod in his direction, she turned and hurried toward the kitchen, where she could occupy herself checking on the staff. Without distractions.

Or maybe she'd take the opportunity to get a grip on herself. Halting just inside the doorway, Paige drew a couple of deep breaths to clear her head and refocus her energies on the client who was paying for this show.

She was doing just that when she suddenly felt a presence behind her, like the other night in the Maitland garden. Siegfried wouldn't have left his table to pursue her, Paige decided. Yet, when she spun around, there he was, so close she nearly bumped into him.

"Siegfried! You can't come in here."

"Why not?"

"Because it's for employees only, and you're a guest." Paige paused, as suspicion struck. "You are a guest, aren't you?"

"I came with the Morrisons," he said.

Although his expression was a bit sheepish, Paige didn't question him further. She was too busy staring at the suit, which looked even better up close and personal.

"You'd better go. Back to the guests, I mean," Paige said, dragging her gaze away from those wide shoulders.

But even as she spoke, she worried how the boy genius would do among the kind of people who called him inept and boorish and looked at him with dollar signs in their eyes. It would be like serving him up on a platter to all the money-hungry females, especially now that he was cleaned up and imminently available.

Once more, Paige felt her protective instincts kick in, and it was all she could do not to call a cab and send him home or to the lab or anywhere such women couldn't get their hands on him. I mean, how often did he venture out into the wide world, especially the cutthroat world of bridesmaids on the prowl?

"Oh, I don't care about them," Siegfried said.

"What?"

"The other guests," he said. "I came to see you." His expression was so guileless that Paige felt that telltale lurch in her chest, which she knew was not good. Hadn't she sworn to deal with Siegfried Maitland on a strictly business level?

"But I'm working." The protest sounded feeble even to Paige.

"Oh. Right," he said, looking disappointed. The poor guy probably didn't realize that most people couldn't come and go as they pleased to secret labs and luxurious offices. Some people had to... *the music!* Paige heard the band begin to play and cursed her own inattention.

"I'm sorry, but I've got things I have to attend to now," she said, seizing her excuse to escape. She stepped outside to see that the bride and groom were already dancing and felt a stab of guilt. She couldn't let the boy genius distract her like this.

"Who's that with you?"

The sound of Zoe's voice in her headset made Paige start.

"Is that Siegfried Maitland?"

"Where are you?" Paige whispered, adjusting her tiny microphone.

"I'm stationed near the top table," Zoe said.

Paige glanced up to see her assistant standing discreetly to the side, with an indiscreet look of curiosity on her face. "Thanks for keeping things moving," she said.

"Oh my God. He's gorgeous."

Paige felt a sharp stab of annoyance. Although Siegfried Maitland wasn't her personal boy toy, here for her sole viewing pleasure, she really didn't want Zoe coming over to work her considerable wiles on the guy.

"Keep your mind on business," she whispered into the headset.

The audience applauded as the bride and groom finished their waltz, and the strains of "The Way You Look Tonight," a perennial favorite at weddings everywhere, began. Since Paige often presented the couple with choices for the special dances, she knew them all by heart.

Privately, she wasn't a big fan of romantic standards, perhaps because familiarity breeds contempt. And Paige knew that most of the starry-eyed couples who swayed to this tune would eventually be facing each other in divorce court, just like her own parents.

It was that knowledge that kept her from getting swept up in the sentimental nonsense that others took to heart. And yet, she found herself listening to the words with less than her usual detachment.

Maybe it was because the guy standing next to her really did look good tonight. Different. Sexy. Manly. Less like a lab dweller, but no less himself. Paige shook her head.

Siegfried was still Siegfried. In fact, he probably had forgotten her very existence and was contemplating how to get his robots to rumba. When she slanted a glance at him, just to check, she found him otherwise occupied all right, but not with his formulas. With a blonde. And not just any blonde. This one was tall and slender, with the best smile and boobs that money could buy.

"Skank alert!"

This time Paige didn't flinch at the sound of Zoe's voice. "Might I remind you that this frequency is for professional use only?" she whispered into her headset.

"I'm just watching your back," Zoe said. "You had better do something before that slut steals your man."

"Zoe," Paige warned.

"Hey, at least do your duty. I'm telling you, the guy looks scared! He's a guest, and you've got to help him."

Paige knew Zoe couldn't see Siegfried's expression from her vantage point. Nor did she imagine the blonde to be particularly frightening.

"I'm sorry," Paige said. "This connection is cancelled." She unhooked the headset and slung it around her neck, trying to look businesslike as she glanced to her right, just for curiosity's sake.

Paige immediately regretted the action. The blonde *was* scary. In fact, she looked like a man-eater who was going to gobble up Siegfried as her next meal. *Over my dead body*, Paige vowed. Unfortunately, she had nothing on her except the headset, which probably wouldn't do much damage, even if used as a weapon.

And that was a good thing, she realized when the shock wave of jealousy had passed. A wedding planner couldn't attack a guest at the reception and expect to get recommendations, even if said guest was intimidating another.

But was she? Siegfried didn't look stricken, only bemused, as though gorgeous, slinky women hit on him every day. Maybe they did. Look at The Maitland Company employees. What if Siegfried had hooked up with all of them? Paige knew the answer: It wasn't any of her business.

Her business was this wedding. And so she watched the dance floor and the attendees and the waitstaff to make sure all was going smoothly. But somehow she couldn't concentrate. The knowledge that Siegfried was nearby—with the blonde cozying up to him—was too distracting.

Determined to take a position somewhere else, Paige glanced once more in that direction and sucked in a deep breath. One moment the woman was leaning forward so that her fake boobs were touching Siegfried's gorgeous suit. The next, she was brushing up against nothing.

Siegfried, being Siegfried, stepped away, grabbed up a napkin, and looked around expectantly, leaving the blonde blinking at thin air. It took Paige a moment to realize he was searching for a pen. And even if the bimbo was aware of what her companion wanted, she wouldn't have anything to help him in her fancy clutch, which was large enough to hold her lipstick and little else.

But Paige had an emergency kit that held extra hosiery, pins, tampons, and anything that the bride or her guests might need, including pens and paper. With cool efficiency, Paige pulled out the writing materials and offered them to Siegfried, who snatched them up immediately.

Paige suppressed a smile as he completely ignored the blonde and sat down in the nearest seat, between a large man and a startled elderly woman. The blonde's initial expression of disbelief turned to annoyance, which she quickly masked as she tried to laugh off Siegfried's defection.

Moving toward him, the skank put her hands on his shoulders and leaned forward to whisper something in his ear, her fake boobs rubbing against his back in a move intended to remind him she was there—and then some. But Siegfried didn't respond, and Paige doubted if he ever would because she knew that look. He wasn't even present, at least not in this dimension.

Paige was tempted to tell the blonde to forget it. After all, the guy was surrounded by young, nubile women at work whom he never even noticed. But before she could say anything, the woman flounced off, looking for fresh prey and leaving Paige with an absurd feeling of triumph.

Siegfried's new position, hunched intently over a notebook, did not invite anyone else to speak to him, and Paige turned her mind back to her work. Yet she kept a wary eye on him as he scribbled away. Although some other guests tried to engage him in conversation throughout the evening, Siegfried barely responded and finally was left alone.

Paige could see how his preoccupation might be construed as rudeness, and each time he was approached, she was tempted to step in. To protect him? To coax him into interacting with others? She wasn't sure what role she should play; she only knew she had an urge to be there, to fix things for him somehow.

It was why she was so good at her job. She wanted to make everything run smoothly, and she succeeded where work was concerned. But life was not so easily managed. It was messy and complicated and couldn't be ordered with notes and schedules and a list of suppliers.

But no one seemed to protest Siegfried's behavior, except perhaps the blonde. Apparently, people were well aware of his reputation. Or, maybe the more rich and famous you were, the more you could get away with. Paige had only to look at Mia Anderson, another scion of the Maitland clan, for an example of that maxim.

So absorbed was he with his writings that Siegfried never even lifted his head when the band packed up and left, the bar closed down, the last guests drifted off, and the waitstaff began cleaning up the empty tables. Finally, only Siegfried remained, and Zoe made Paige swear not to desert him.

"If you don't step in, he might be here come morning," her assistant whispered in amazement.

Paige wasn't about to abandon the guy. As she watched his dark head bent over his work, an unexpected lump formed in her throat. She swallowed hard against it and moved toward him. Would he even listen to her? He'd pretty much ignored everyone else, including the poor woman whose seat he had commandeered.

Stepping closer, Paige cleared her throat but got no reaction. "Siegfried? It's time to go," she said softly.

He didn't even blink. Resisting the urge to lean over him as the blonde had done, Paige knelt beside him and put a hand on his sleeve. "Siegfried," she said, surprised at the catch in her voice.

At last, he turned his head and saw her. His expression of

concentration cleared, his gorgeous lips curved, and his eyes grew wide, as if in wonder.

"Paige." His deep voice was full of something, surprise maybe, but not annoyance. And the way he stared at her made Paige feel like they were the only two people there. Well, maybe they were, but it seemed like they were the only two people in the world.

Although his shaggy hair was falling into his eyes and his tie was askew, somehow he looked better than ever. There was a starry sky above and the scent of flowers in the air, and Paige just might have done something stupid if it hadn't been for the guy who was waiting to take away the tablecloth.

"Excuse me," the waiter said, reaching out for it.

Whatever weird spell she was under was broken, and Paige rose to her feet, snatching up Siegfried's papers before they could end up in the trash. She turned to hand him what she had collected only to find him looking at her again, really intently.

"Do you need..." Paige's words trailed off, and she sucked in some air to steady herself. "... a ride home?"

When Siegfried eyed her blankly, Paige realized how stupid her question must sound. Obviously, the Maitland heir had not gotten here by skateboard.

"Oh, your driver is probably around here somewhere. Do you need to call him or something?" Paige asked. She looked around, as if Arthur were going to pop out of the bushes at any moment. But she didn't see any expensive cars, just her old subcompact and what looked like staff parking.

"A ride would be good," Siegfried said.

Spoken in his low voice, the words took on a new meaning, and Paige found herself blushing in a totally unbusinesslike manner. She wondered if this was a bad idea, but what else could she do? The guy appeared to have no vehicle, and she suspected he had no money and no phone, either.

"I let Arthur go home," he said.

So now Paige had no choice, unless she wanted to leave her

richest client at a deserted venue, waiting for a driver who might or might not be reliable, considering the typical Maitland employee. But somehow Paige didn't feel the expected annoyance at the imposition, only a curious sort of elation, which couldn't be good.

"Just let me get everything," she muttered.

Grabbing her stuff, Paige motioned toward her car. Siegfried loaded in her things, which just drew her attention to his shoulders again. It had to be the suit that made him look so good, Paige decided, trying not to notice.

She also tried not to notice how good he smelled when she was trapped inside her car with him in the dark. Studiously avoiding looking at him, Paige watched the road instead, but somehow San Francisco at night had never seemed so romantic or her passenger more attractive.

And why was that stupid song from the reception stuck in her head?

CHAPTER THIRTEEN

The drive out to the estate seemed to grow shorter with each trip, and when the familiar gates appeared, Paige felt a welcoming glow that she promptly dismissed. Just because she had been here more than once did not give her any claim to the place. She went to lots of elegant residences, mostly as wedding venues, of course, but there was no reason for her to feel any special attachment to this one.

Maybe the Maitland mansion appealed to her because the solid Tudor design made it appear to have stood here for longer than it had. There was a sense of history about the house and at the same time a bit of whimsy, as though it was a magical place crafted out of fantasies.

Paige frowned at the memory of the wedding guest calling it "ghastly." The building just needed a little work, and it could be someone's dream home again.

Paige deliberately headed up the curving drive toward the lights at the main entrance. As much as she liked the house, she was not going to pull into the garages and get talked into going inside. She told herself there was nothing for her in there except Mia's acerbic tongue. Okay, and maybe Siegfried's clever one.

Slamming on the brakes, Paige put the car in park, only to realize he was there in the dark beside her, smelling good and looking even better. The enclosed space grew warm, and was it her imagination, or had her already small vehicle shrunk in size? Pushing open her door, Paige stepped out and drew in a deep breath.

Unfortunately, she was greeted by the same night air that had seduced her the last time she had been here. Try as she might to avoid it, the memory of the kiss came rushing back, and Paige realized the front of the house wasn't much safer than the gardens.

The old-fashioned lighting out here was dim, making for a

moonlit type atmosphere as her companion rose from the car, tall and handsome and wearing that great suit. Paige swallowed. At least the vehicle was between them.

But not for long. As she stood there clutching the door handle, Siegfried walked around the car, away from the entrance to the house, and toward her. Maybe it was the clothes, but for someone who was so often awkward and gawky, he moved pretty, uh, smoothly. Paige turned to face him, her back against the metal as though to ward off any romantic nonsense.

But, in typical Siegfried fashion, the guy did not mention the moon or the night or the way she filled out her own little black dress.

"You left the engine on," he stated baldly.

"I know. I've got to get going," Paige said, feeling for the handle behind her.

"You're not coming in?" he asked. His open expression showed puzzlement. Or was it disappointment? Paige's heart began a wild rhythm of temptation.

"No. I can't," Paige said, turning away. But when she moved, he lifted an arm as though reaching for her. Maybe he wanted to drag her into the house with him, or maybe he was just going to open the door for her. But that's not how things turned out.

Before Paige knew it, she was caught between a rock and a hard place, or more accurately, between a car and a hard guy. Then came the kiss, and she wanted to melt right into the cobbled stones at her feet.

Some lingering sliver of sanity told her she wasn't supposed to be doing this. But why? Her long-deprived body protested.

Oh, yeah. Because this was Siegfried Maitland, boy genius, billionaire, and client. Paige broke away from those luscious lips and murmured against his cheek.

"I really have to be going."

"Hmm." His response was more a grunt than anything else, made while his mouth moved along the sensitive skin of her neck. Paige didn't think it had a thing to do with what she had just said, but was more of a comment on his explorations, which he seemed to find gratifying. Paige sure did.

"Really. I've got to go," she said, a bit breathlessly, as she leaned her head to the side to give him better access.

"Hmm." And then somehow he had managed to undo the tiny buttons at the back of her dress, causing it to gape open and reveal her black bra.

"How did that happen?" she whispered.

"I'm good with my hands," he murmured. "Manual dexterity." He smiled, and all thoughts of going home fled from Paige's mind. Instead, she tilted her face up to meet his, her fingers grasping his thick hair.

He was using one of those amazing hands to investigate her bra when light flooded them. It was definitely a déjà vu moment, and Paige vowed right then and there to murder Mia Anderson if she was gloating on the front steps.

But it was a man's voice that rang out in the brightness. "Who's out there?" Arthur, the chauffeur-cum-watchman, called loudly from the direction of the garages.

A frantic fumbling with her clothes brought Paige's dress up over her chest, although it still hung open at the back. Not wanting to be caught out by the driver, in case he came to investigate, Paige grasped the handle behind her, opened the door, and squeezed inside her car.

She had a glimpse of Siegfried's face, outside the glass, and he looked so lost that she cracked down the window so he could hear her. "I've got to go!" she said.

When had a guy ever looked so guileless? Before his expression could change her mind, Paige closed the window and put the car in gear. It was hard to peel rubber on cobblestones, but she did her best, racing away from the Maitland estate as if the devil himself were after her.

Although there was nothing really devilish about Siegfried, Paige couldn't still her sense of panic, as if she were losing control of herself and her carefully ordered existence. And the boy genius was to blame.

Paige juggled a large peppermint mocha cappuccino, an even larger cookie, her bag, and her door key. Naturally, since she had no free hands, her cell started ringing. She managed to insert the key, turn the lock, dump everything on the counter, and still catch the caller on the last ring.

"Hello?" she said a bit breathlessly.

"Can you talk?" Zoe's voice was a whisper.

"Yes. I was just getting in the door," Paige answered, shutting it behind her.

"So he's not there with you?"

"Who?" Paige asked, although she could hazard a guess as to Zoe's meaning.

"Siegfried Maitland, of course."

"No, he's not with me," Paige said, annoyed. "Is he supposed to be?"

"Where are you?"

"At home!"

"So what happened?"

"Nothing," Paige said. Well, almost nothing. "I took him back to the estate."

"That's not nothing. So? Did you get to see the gold-plated bathroom fixtures and, more importantly, the Egyptian sheets?"

"No! Look, Zoe, I told you that I'm not starting anything up with Siegfried Maitland," Paige said.

"So he didn't invite you in?" Zoe sounded suspicious.

"No. Yes. I don't know." Paige hedged.

Zoe snorted. "You don't know? That means he did, and you didn't. Why not?"

"Look, Zoe, I don't know why you insist on pushing me into something that makes me uncomfortable," Paige said, tossing her keys in her purse.

There. She had said it. She was uncomfortable with Siegfried's attention, delicious though it might be. Who would have thought that the skateboarder-cum-computer whiz would be so hot? So gentle? So good with his hands?

"Hello? How long has it been since you've had sex?" Zoe asked. The question jarred Paige from the thoughts that had kept her tossing and turning all night and had sent her out early for coffee on what should have been a lazy morning.

After all those hours of dissecting what had happened, Paige could only come to one conclusion. As much as she had enjoyed Siegfried Maitland's manual dexterity, she wasn't about to take advantage of it again.

Acutely aware of Zoe on the other end of the line, Paige grabbed up her cappuccino while trying to avoid her assistant's question. As far as she was concerned, it was not germane to the issue.

"You can't remember, can you?" Zoe said. "If you can't remember, then it has been way too long. Here's your opportunity to end the drought with a really eligible bachelor, so seize your chance with both hands."

Zoe laughed at her own joke. "And if the quiet one doesn't know what to do, then you can teach him. Hey, you can train him up the right way!"

"He doesn't need any instruction," Paige muttered before catching herself.

"What?" Zoe fairly shrieked. "What did you do? Don't tell me you did it at the reception?"

"Please tell me you are not out in public while we're having this conversation," Paige said. "And I certainly did not do it at one of my weddings," she added, sinking into the nearest chair.

"Then you didn't do it? At all?"

Zoe was like a dog with a bone, so Paige eventually spilled the truth, or at least a version of it. There was no way she was going to admit just how much she had enjoyed herself or the way the look on Siegfried's face had affected her. Guys just didn't look like that, not ones past the age of five anyway.

"I hate to keep repeating myself, but why didn't you just go in with him?" Zoe asked.

"It's too complicated," Paige said. Taking a sip of cappuccino, she swirled the hot drink around on her tongue and remembered how much better Siegfried tasted. The unwelcome thought made her jump to her feet, and she dumped the whole thing in the sink.

"So un-complicate it," Zoe said.

Paige sighed."I told you before that it's just too difficult with him being part of the biggest project we've ever had," she said. "If he were some regular guy I met at a club, it would be different."

"Oh, yeah. Like you're into casual sex. And when was the last time you went to a club?"

Zoe didn't wait for Paige to answer. "I think you're scared. This is the first guy who's gotten to you in ages, if ever. And you're afraid of feeling something for him, something you can't manage like you do everything else."

"I don't know what you're talking about," Paige said, tossing the cup in the trash with a little extra force.

"Hello? Can we say control freak? That's an affliction that works well when you're planning other people's weddings, but what about your own? Some of the best things in life are stuff we have no control over. Like Siegfried Maitland."

Paige snorted. Siegfried was uncontrollable, that was certain. By all accounts, the guy couldn't keep track of appointments or even feed himself properly. The thought immediately made her wonder when he had his last meal, a concern she forced herself to ignore.

You never knew what the guy would do, invite you to jump out of an airplane or disappear into another dimension. It was mind-boggling.

"I do not like unpredictability, spontaneity, or any of those other i-t-y words you're always trying to push on me," Paige said. Responsibility was the only -ity that interested her.

And that meant concentrating on her business, maybe doing some casual dating, but not taking on Siegfried Maitland. Client or not, the guy would be a full-time job in itself. Just dragging him out of the lab would be an effort.

"You don't know him, Zoe. He's not like other people,"

Paige said. "It would be like having a kid! I'd be a caretaker, not a girlfriend."

"If you say so," Zoe said. "But I'm sure the poor, abnormal guy can find plenty of other women willing to take care of him, like that blonde at the reception."

Paige felt a burst of jealousy that had her grasping the phone in a death grip. Thankfully, she retained enough sense to see it for what it was: just the sort of thing she didn't need— messy, emotional crap that led to life mistakes. Like the ones her mom had made.

"Well, better her than me, then," Paige said. "I've got to go." Ending the call, she turned off the phone, along with all thoughts of Siegfried Maitland.

And she was in control again, at least for awhile.

CHAPTER FOURTEEN

For the next few days, Paige watched her calls closely, planning to avoid any further contact with the boy genius. Every time the Maitland number came up, she composed herself and prepared to be polite yet firm, just in case it was him. But it was always someone else from the house with wedding suggestions, and Paige grew annoyed.

Okay, maybe she had decided not to have anything more to do with Siegfried, but he didn't know that. So why hadn't he called? Because he probably was buried in the lab, not eating or sleeping, Paige decided. Obviously, the guy never thought of her unless she was standing a foot from him—and sometimes not even then.

The notion stung, and she wanted to strangle Zoe, with her meddling encouragement. Thankfully, Paige had refused to listen. What was there to be encouraging about?

So Siegfried had kissed her. Big deal. He probably kissed whoever was handy when the urge struck him. Like skydiving and skateboarding, it was just another whim and meant nothing. Now Paige was glad she had escaped with nothing worse than a bruised ego. Like Zoe said, she wasn't into casual sex, and a hookup without even a call afterward would make her feel like a slut.

And since she would be seeing Siegfried again, the situation really would have been awkward. Paige congratulated herself on her good sense in not following Zoe's advice and vowed never to listen to her friend in the future.

The sad truth was that Siegfried Maitland forgot her the second she was out of sight. And that knowledge made her even more determined to avoid him.

Although calls from the estate continued, they were never from Siegfried, and Paige might have wondered whether he even knew how to use a phone—if she cared. Which she didn't.

Meanwhile, the Maitlands' cook had taken to calling nearly every morning to see whether Paige would be joining the family for dinner, even though her answer was always negative.

A couple of weeks later, Paige was still fielding the question and juggling the suggestions of mansion residents. By the time the third call came in, she debated whether to answer it or let it go to voice mail. The businesswoman in her made her pick up, and if her heart was beating in an unbusinesslike manner, that abated as soon as she heard Bebe's voice.

"Oh, Paige, dear! I'm so glad I was able to reach you," the older woman said.

"Thank you. It's always nice to talk to you, too," Paige said. And she meant it. She didn't hold the boy genius against his grandmother.

"We have a little problem here that I'm hoping you can help us with. Can you please come out right away?"

Great. Paige loosed a sigh. What was the emergency this time? Was Linde complaining about her bridesmaid's dress again?

"Are you sure I can't solve things from here? I've got kind of a hectic schedule," Paige said. "Can you just put Linde on the phone?"

"Whyever for, dear? She has nothing to do with this."

So Hilde was the difficulty? Paige gritted her teeth. "All right. I'll be there in an hour."

Mentally, Paige was already rescheduling her appointments, even as she dialed Zoe. It was a good thing they had hired some additional help. The Maitland nuptials were beginning to suck up more and more of her time.

Paige told herself that all the personal attention she was giving her wealthiest client would be worth it in the end as she made the drive out to the Maitland home once more. The sight of the familiar place always managed to soothe her, as if the house were reaching out in welcome. Which was more than she got from Godfrey when he opened the door.

The butler acknowledged her with a lift of his white brows. "Ms. Porter. Here again, I see," he said.

"Aren't you happy to see me?" Paige asked, lifting her own brows.

"Overjoyed," he said dryly. "But, as you are becoming such a frequent visitor, I thought I might invite you to access the house through one of the family entrances."

For some reason the invitation made Paige feel all cheery inside, even though she knew it was not a sign of affection.

"What? Too lazy to do your job?" she asked.

"It does become a bit tiresome," he answered stoically.

Paige laughed out loud. There was something heart-warming about the stiff, British butler, something that made her wish she really was part of the family and could enter through their private doors, enjoying a sense of belonging she had never known. She blinked abruptly at the thought, and then Bebe was upon her in a cloud of perfume.

"Oh, dear, I'm so glad you're here. I just didn't know who else to turn to," Bebe said, looking flustered.

Paige eyed her carefully. Maybe this was more personal than she had thought. "I'm happy to help in whatever way I can. Sit down, and tell me what's worrying you," Paige said, leading the older woman to a chair.

"Oh no. Not here, dear," Bebe said. "We have to go to the basement."

Paige's heart lurched in her chest. Had something happened in the lab? To Siegfried? Hadn't his father or his grandfather blown himself up with some invention gone awry?

She sucked in a breath as she followed Bebe, but they didn't head toward the elevator. Instead, the older woman led her to the kitchen, where they passed a large woman who glared at them as though protecting her turf.

"Oh, Cook, you remember Paige, don't you?" Bebe said.

Cook? Didn't the woman have a name?

The woman nodded, though Paige didn't recall ever meeting her before. "I see you'll be here for dinner after all," she said.

Paige shook her head but hurried to follow Bebe. Where were they going, to a wine cellar? Maybe some private stock intended for the wedding had gone bad or been pilfered.

It was a wonder the Maitlands weren't robbed blind the way they invited everyone into their home. What good were the gates, if Bebe let everyone in? The only real security was Tad way down in the lab.

The thought made Paige worry about Siegfried again. Maybe there was another entrance to his lair from the basement, but Paige couldn't remember seeing any. Then again, she had been a bit preoccupied at the time because the guy was carrying her. Flushing at the memory, Paige steadied herself as they reached the bottom of the stairs.

The basement was cool and clean and relatively normal-looking to someone from the Midwest. They were an unusual feature in California, but obviously not for the very rich, for Paige saw a well-stocked wine cellar behind a locked grate.

But that's not where Bebe led her. Instead, the matriarch brought her face-to-face with an ancient metal monstrosity. Obviously, this part of the basement was not as up-to-date as the lab.

"It's the furnace," Bebe said.

Paige couldn't argue. But why, exactly, were they staring at it?

"It won't work," Bebe said.

Paige looked from the society matron to the metal behemoth, and back again. Of course, this was Wackyland, so why should she be surprised that she had been summoned to the estate not to solve a wedding crisis, but to fix the furnace?

"Naturally, we won't freeze, but it does get cool at night, and, well, I've had some complaints. Lorenzo is used to a warmer clime, you know," Bebe said.

Lorenzo was probably from New Jersey, but Paige didn't comment. She just wondered what the heck she was supposed to do. She was the wedding planner, a small matter that seemed to have escaped Bebe's notice.

She turned toward the older woman. "Why don't you ask Siegfried to take a look at it?"

Bebe laughed. "Oh my, no. This is far too low-tech to interest him."

Paige gritted her teeth. Like a typical male, the boy genius was utterly useless, even if he could be coaxed away from his work. "Well, I don't know a thing about them, but I can call a repairman," Paige said.

"Oh, thank you. That would be lovely, dear," Bebe said. While Paige trailed behind, biting her tongue and musing on the vagaries of the very rich, Bebe led her back upstairs.

As they made their way through the house Paige wondered whether she ought to hint that this normally was not part of her job. If Bebe expected her to trot out here for every household problem, she would never be able to keep up with her real business.

Paige was trying to decide just what to say when Bebe swung open the door to an unfamiliar room. Small compared to the rest of the house, it was nonetheless quite spacious. And the sight of it made Paige swallow her speech.

A beautifully appointed office, it was done in creams and pale pastels with elegant furniture that was not too heavy, but delicate and feminine. And beyond the furnishings, tall Tudor windows looked out over the sea.

Paige drew in a sharp breath.

"You can call from here, dear," Bebe said. "In fact, you can use this room whenever you are at the house. It belonged to my personal assistant, but we didn't work well together."

Paige was too busy admiring the place to reply. There was even a top-of-the-line computer system, discreetly hidden in a cupboard behind the desk. Dazed, Paige sank into a chair and let out a sigh at its comfort. How did it manage to be both beautiful and ergonomic? She pulled open a drawer, and stationery with the Maitland letterhead stared up at her.

"I could get used to this," she whispered. But when she glanced up, embarrassed to have spoken aloud, she saw that

Bebe had gone, having closed the door behind her.

Alone now, Paige studied the place more closely. She and Zoe had talked about opening an office, but rental prices were so steep, they couldn't afford anything that would impress.

So they met clients at their homes or prospective venues or vendors, worked out of their apartments, and kept any paper files, decorations, materials, etc., at the home of Zoe's parents. As her gaze wandered lovingly around the room, Paige saw a couple of doors, which probably concealed plenty of storage space.

Focus, Paige, she told herself. She had everything she needed on her laptop and phone. She certainly didn't require a scenario out of a magazine spread in which to make her calls. But it sure would be nice.

With a rueful smile, Paige reminded herself she was here not as an owner or even as a temporary resident, but as an employee. Swinging round, she typed in a search for a repair company and made the call. Then she leaned back in her chair and looked out the windows. The sight made her loose a deep sigh.

Cost of gas to drive up here? Too much. Medicine to deal with headache-inducing residents? Cheap. But the views? *Priceless.*

A light tapping at the door interrupted her solitude. Who knew she was here? Was Siegfried even in residence today? Paige cleared her throat. "Come in," she called. She looked up hopefully, but it was only Lila, the multi-pierced maid.

"Hey," she said, brandishing a tray. "Thought you could use a break."

Before Paige could question what she was taking a break from—her trifling errand, the Maitland household, or thoughts of its owner—Lila set the tray down on the desk. Spread out on it was a plate of gourmet cookies, a diet cola, and a glass full of ice.

Paige swallowed hard against a sudden lump in her throat at the thoughtful gesture. She had never been pampered. Her mother had been too busy working, and Paige had been on her own for years, carving out a career with very few perks.

Now, here she was being treated to a beautiful office, a gorgeous view, and indulgences that rivaled anything from the local coffee shop. They had even remembered her diet cola.

Who could ask for anything more?

Paige told herself not to answer that question for fear of where it might lead. Instead, she tried to get Lila to take a cookie, but the maid swore she never ate refined sugar.

"I hope you're here longer than the last one," Lila said. She paused to eye Paige up and down. "But you look like you can handle it."

What was the girl talking about? Paige had thought Lila one of the more normal people to be found at the Maitland estate, body piercings notwithstanding.

"The last one?" Paige said. "Did Hilde have another wedding planner?"

Now it was Lila's turn to look confused. "No. I'm talking about Bebe's assistant."

Paige blinked. "I'm afraid I'm just the wedding planner."

"Yeah, right," Lila said. "Bebe said you were to use the office as long as you like, whenever you like, and I was to get you anything you need." She grinned as if resting her case. "Do you need anything else?"

Paige shook her head slowly.

"Great. So I'll let you know when the repair guy gets here," she said. Without waiting for a response, she walked out and shut the door.

Paige was left staring dumbly after her. Okay. Apparently, she had to hang around here for awhile. But that shouldn't be a problem. She had her phone. She could access her schedule and make some calls, get some prices, verify some dates, etc. In fact, she could do almost everything here and enjoy it far more than in her own cramped quarters.

With a grin, Paige poured herself the diet cola and leaned back in her incredibly comfy chair, more than happy to enjoy the Maitland hospitality.

CHAPTER FIFTEEN

Having mastered the state-of-the-art computer, Paige was studying caterers' menus online when another knock came on the door. Thinking Lila was back, she called out a welcome, but it was Godfrey who stood on the threshold. And he announced in snooty tones that a Mr. Rodriguez was here to see her.

"Who?" Paige asked, still focused on her work.

"Mr. Rodriguez," the butler said. "He states that he is a representative of Bay Plumbing and Heating."

"Oh, right." Paige glanced away from the screen. "Can you show him to the furnace?"

Godfrey gave her a look, which she returned. What did the guy do, if not direct visitors?

"I'm afraid I'm not familiar with the situation," Godfrey said.

"You're just as familiar as I am," Paige said. "In fact, I don't see why you couldn't have called him yourself."

The butler looked down his proper British nose at her, his voice decidedly haughty when he spoke. "It's not in my job description."

"And it's in mine?" Paige asked.

Godfrey lifted his white brows."You're the one in the office."

"That doesn't make me Bebe's assistant," Paige said. Not that there was anything wrong with being Bebe's assistant, but Paige had her own business to run.

"Don't tell me. Let me guess," the butler said, with a deadpan expression. "You were kidnapped from whatever pitiful closet you call home, forced to inspect the furnace here, and are now being held captive in this luxurious space."

Busted. Paige glanced up at him with a rueful smile. Maybe the Maitlands were blamed unfairly for their historic eccentricity. "It's the house, isn't it?" she said. "It makes people do crazy things."

The butler's lips curved slightly. "By the way, I should be remiss if I didn't inform you that your office has its own powder room and an adjoining room that can be turned into a bedroom, if desired."

What? Was Godfrey suggesting that Paige move in here, to live rent free in one of the most famous private residences in the area, running her own business out of this spacious, elegant room, while enjoying gratis maid and room service?

"Right," Paige muttered to herself.

That was *so* not going to happen.

By the time the repairman had completed his work, advising Paige to replace the aging unit, it was late and she was expected to stay for dinner. Paige paid him from a folder of checks provided by Bebe, then turned to the older woman to ask the question that had been lingering at the back of her mind all day.

"Is, uh, Siegfried here?" Not that she wanted to see him or anything. The guy obviously had no clue about how to behave or any kind of date etiquette. Not that they'd ever been on a date.

"I have no idea, dear. We haven't seen him in days," Bebe said, dismissing her grandson with a wave of her hand.

"Aren't you concerned?" Paige asked.

"Oh my, no," Bebe said. "It's not uncommon for him to disappear for weeks at a time."

"Doesn't anyone check on him?"

"No, dear. He doesn't like to be disturbed," Bebe said.

Paige frowned. She supposed that's how it went with geniuses. One day they were fondling you, the next day they were fondling robots. The thought that Siegfried might actually prefer the robots was depressing—even if she didn't plan on any future fondling with him.

And what kind of guy wouldn't let his own family know whether he was alive or dead? What if he were ill or hadn't eaten? Did he sleep down in the lab?

Paige felt a surge of protectiveness, which she quickly stifled. She shouldn't be concerned whether the guy starved himself or not; she should just take care of business. Then again, taking care of Siegfried might qualify as business, considering that he was paying for the event of the year.

Paige paused, uncertain. Hey, she was here, so she might as well make sure the guy was okay. Right?

"If you like, I could, uh, check and see if he wants to join us," Paige suggested. She expected another demure, but Bebe was delighted.

"Oh, would you, dear? We would be so grateful!"

So Paige found herself taking the elevator down to the lab and trying not to picture her last trip in it—when she was cradled against Siegfried's tall body. Warm. Safe. Breathless.

And soon forgotten, she reminded herself.

The doors opened suddenly, and Paige blinked against the brightness of the white and chrome lab, a stark contrast to the often dark interior of the house. She squinted, searching for Siegfried among the banks of computers and metal tables. This time she noticed several glassed-in areas housing the robots themselves, like some kind of creepy sci-fi offices.

"Hey, you! Stop right there!"

Paige immediately recognized the voice of the burly guard who had tried to keep her out before, and one glimpse told her he was about to do the same now. Stepping into the lab, Paige glanced around, hoping to find Siegfried while she still had a chance.

Luckily, she saw him before Tad reached her, but the boy genius was slumped over one of the monitors, looking as though he hadn't slept in a week. His hair was more rumpled than usual, his clothes were impossible, and his face had the shadows of a beard. Okay, that was sexy. But his eyes were so red-rimmed, he might have been shooting up.

Without thinking, Paige squatted down beside him like she had at the wedding. "Siegfried! Are you okay?"

He turned his head slowly and blinked at her, as though

slow to focus, but when recognition dawned, his expression changed. His face softened, his eyes widened, his mouth curved into a smile, and Paige's heart lurched.

For a long moment, she didn't know how to respond. She just kept staring at Siegfried while he stared back. He was watching her as though she were the most wonderful thing he had ever seen, and Paige was dangerously close to feeling the same way about him.

"Step away from the monitor."

Tad's command jarred her from her stupor, and Paige rose to her feet, half expecting the guard to be holding a gun on her. Thankfully, he was not. But he looked menacing enough without one.

"It's all right, Tad," Siegfried said. The weariness in his voice sent her heart lurching again and made her want to smack the security guard.

"No, it's not, sir," Tad said. "This woman should not have access to the lab."

"Bebe wanted me to come get Siegfried for dinner, or is feeding him against the rules of the lockdown?" Paige asked, temper flaring. "This man is the owner of the house and your boss, not a prisoner!"

Tad ignored her. "I've told you before, sir. We need to restrict access to the lab."

"I'm sure no one's going to get past you, Tad," Siegfried said, pushing away from the monitor to stand beside Paige. He dragged a hand over his face.

"Maybe I should get a shower first," he said, lifting his dark brows in a rueful expression.

"Food first. Shower later," Paige said. "I promised Bebe, you know."

Personally, she was afraid he'd fall asleep under the spray and drown himself. So what if he was a little haggard-looking? He didn't stink or anything. Okay, maybe a little, but underneath the stale odor of sweat was that delicious Siegfried smell.

Paige shook her head as she followed him into the elevator. Maybe she was the one who needed a shower—an extremely cold one.

Once the doors shut in front of them, Paige was at a loss for words. Obviously, she didn't need to ask how he'd been since he looked so awful. And what he'd been doing was obvious, too: overworking and under-eating. And not showering. Okay, maybe she should get off the water imagery before she offered to wash him herself.

Paige sucked in a deep breath.

Of course, there was another nagging question that remained unspoken: Did you forget all about me? But Paige knew better than to go there. She was here on business, she told herself. And anything else just wasn't her business.

With that in mind, Paige tried to keep her professional focus all during dinner even though she had been accorded a seat right beside the Maitland heir. So she was the one who kept having to nudge him to eat when he looked like he was going to doze off.

Maybe an IV would have been better, so he could eat and sleep at the same time, Paige thought, wondering whether the guy was just exhausted or really ill. Maybe he had some kind of genius condition she didn't know about.

"Poor Siegfried," Uncle Otto said, nodding toward the end of the table. "The boy works too hard."

"You've seen him like this before?" Paige asked.

"Oh yes," Otto said. "Not all the time, of course, but when he becomes obsessed with an idea, a breakthrough, as he says, then he will work himself too much. His papa was the same way, but his mama would take care to prevent too much work, just as you must do."

The older man paused to smile at Paige in an alarming fashion that made her shake her head in denial. She would have protested aloud, but she had a mouthful of veal, and she couldn't eat, talk, and feed Siegfried at the same time.

"He needs his rest," Otto said. "First you feed him, then you must put him to bed."

Paige nearly choked at that advice, but she was sure the

man had intended no double entendre. After all, he hadn't told her to take Siegfried to bed, just put him there. So why were images of the former dancing in her head? Paige flushed. Was it hot in here?

"I'm sure you or Bebe should do that," Paige said, reaching for her water goblet.

"Oh no!" Otto shook his head. "He does not like us to interfere, ever since he was the young one."

Great, Paige thought. Had she just blown her goodwill with the guy by dragging him from his lab? Her brow furrowing, she snuck a glance at her companion. He was chewing like a narcoleptic going down for the count, while on her left, Otto patted her arm.

"Ah, but with you, it is not interfering, yes?" he asked.

"I'm sure that he—" Paige began, but she never finished because she could see Siegfried pitching forward. Jumping to her feet, Paige managed to catch him before he landed face first in the saffron cream sauce.

So they skipped dessert. No brandy. No coffee. No conversation. In fact, some people were still eating when Paige helped Siegfried to his feet and dragged him toward the door.

It wasn't until he was leaning on her in the hall, one arm heavily around her shoulders, his slightly sweaty Siegfried scent filling her senses, that Paige wondered what to do next.

Thankfully, Godfrey appeared before the guy could collapse, and Paige tried to hand responsibility for the employer over to the employee. "Godfrey, could you please help Siegfried to his room? He's a bit, uh, tired," Paige said.

Godfrey lifted his bushy brows to eye both of them askance. "I'm afraid that at my age, I cannot support anything heavy," the butler said. "But I would be happy to direct you to where you may deposit your burden."

Paige knew better than to argue, so she simply followed Godfrey through the house and up the grand stair. "This way, please," the butler said. "Mr. Siegfried has a private wing, though he makes little use of it."

A private wing? Wasn't this a "private" house? Then again,

it sometimes seemed like an institution for the terminally wacky, so Paige said nothing. Finally, Godfrey swung open a set of heavily carved double doors that led into a thickly carpeted, wide hallway where she assumed Siegfried had a bedroom, instead of a lab cot.

When Godfrey opened another elaborate door and gestured for her to step inside, Paige drew in a sharp breath and wondered how anyone would want to sleep anywhere else. Ever.

It was a bedroom suite that Zoe would die for, Paige thought as she took in the elegance, the spaciousness, the luxurious carpet, and the huge four-poster. Like most of the house, the room needed some improving, but there were perfect gems like the tiled fireplace and the tall windows covered by old-fashioned, heavy drapes, that just might look out over the ocean.

Paige sighed in admiration, only to realize that she was standing there staring, while Siegfried grew heavier and heavier. She turned her head to find his handsome face, stubble and all, just inches from her own.

"Did you still want a shower?" she asked. Somehow, the words came out in a sultry whisper, and she cleared her throat, looking at Godfrey in desperation. "Could you give him a hand?"

She should have known better.

The butler lifted his bushy brows. "I beg your pardon? I am not his valet."

"He has a valet?"

"No, he does not," Godfrey said. "So I suggest that you assist him."

"Me?" Paige asked in what sounded like a squeak. She didn't dare look at Siegfried. "Maybe you should just go to bed," she told him, although she would have liked to find out for Zoe whether the faucets were gold plated. Instead, she led the boy genius to the deliciously high bed and its thick duvet, probably with a one million thread count.

"Good idea," Siegfried mumbled as he sat down on the edge. Before she could comment, he stretched out, grabbed the pillow, and hugged it to him. In a moment, he was breathing deeply.

He was so much like a kid, dropping off so quickly and clinging to his pillow, Paige thought. And yet the dark signs of a beard proclaimed that he was no boy. Sucking in a breath at the realization, she fought an urge to push that overgrown hair back from his brow.

Be professional. Paige's inner voice spoke so loudly that she thought Godfrey had said something, probably snarky, while she was mooning over his boss. But when she swung round, she saw that the butler had left the room, closing the double doors behind him.

Great. Was she supposed to babysit or, worse yet, crawl in beside the boy genius? The very thought set Paige's heart pounding in anticipation, but she was supposed to be avoiding him, right?

And, anyway, the poor guy needed some rest. With a sigh, Paige turned off the phone by the bed. She glanced at the prone body but didn't trust herself to pat him down to look for a cell, which he wasn't supposed to have anyway.

Tearing herself away from the sight of him, Paige told herself that no matter what others in this house might think, her job was to take care of weddings, not Siegfried Maitland. Minding him wasn't her business.

But she kept worrying about him, long after she had left the Maitland mansion for her apartment. Much later, when ensconced in her own pull-out bed, she told herself that rescuing the guy from his lab, feeding him, and getting him some sleep was more than enough.

She couldn't very well stand guard at the door or crawl in with him, even if the bed was more than big enough for both of them. And way more comfortable than her own.

She simply didn't belong there.

So why did she keep thinking of the gorgeous office that smelled of fresh flowers and polished wood, and Siegfried, who smelled of... Siegfried? If only she could shake the memory of his expression when he saw her in the lab, his brown eyes wide, his dark brows lifted in surprise, and that smile.

Paige's heart pounded so hard that he had to remind herself that before that moment, the guy had probably forgotten her existence.

And that's what she wanted. Right?

It began with the furnace but certainly didn't end there. Somehow, Paige found herself supervising the purchase of an entirely new heating system for the estate, along with all her other responsibilities.

She thrived on work, so it wasn't really a problem, especially when she delegated more of her other duties to Zoe and the new hire. Of course, her involvement necessitated a presence at the estate, so she ended up using the rooms provided. And why not?

Who wouldn't want to work in a magazine-spread type of environment rather than a cramped apartment? Who wouldn't prefer to be waited on hand and foot in return for doing a bit of organizing, which came as naturally to her as breathing?

And if she caught a glimpse of the boy genius, well, that was just an added perk. Not that she was actively seeking him out or anything.

Soon the space began to take on her personality, and Paige became more familiar with the residents of the house. Before she knew it, she was making doctor appointments for Uncle Otto, scheduling Bebe's charity work, and booking Lorenzo's travel. In fact, Paige became the unofficial go-to girl for everyone in the household—everyone, that is, except Siegfried.

The boy genius had been sucked back into his lab. Actually, for the past week or so, he'd been away in Geneva or Japan or someplace, hobnobbing with his fellow robot wizards. Paige wondered if he took an assistant with him or his team and whether any of them made him eat or sleep right—or with them.

Paige dismissed the thought and tried to concentrate on her accounts, but this afternoon Linde was at it again. Paige could hear the caterwauling even in her office, and she cringed in response. But she hated to close the door. When it was open, people popped in or stopped by to chat. It was like being in a workplace without the stress of the politics or like being self-employed without the isolation.

It was almost as if she were part of a family, Paige thought, with sudden insight. A really weird family, she added, as she longed for some earplugs.

Finally, she got up and walked to the doorway, flinching as the singing grew louder. Since it wasn't her house, she could hardly yell at Linde to keep it down, so her only options were to close the door or leave.

Paige glanced at her watch and was mentally rearranging her schedule, when the sound was cut off abruptly. Breathing a sigh of relief, she drew it back in as the would-be opera singer rounded the corner.

"Paige! I see that you were listening," Linde said, looking pleased to catch her standing in the doorway. She stopped and made an expansive gesture with her arms, which caused the sleeves of her gown to waft through the air like butterfly wings. It was an odd effect for a woman who couldn't be much older than Paige. Where did the girl get her clothes?

"Well?" Linde asked. "What did you think?"

It took Paige a minute to realize the girl was talking about her singing, not her outfit. Either way, Paige was going to have to do some quick thinking. "Oh. I'm not much of an opera fan," she said, in the understatement of the year.

Linde eyed her with contempt. "It's *Ave Maria*," she said. "For the wedding."

Paige didn't know how to react. She had heard the piece sung many times at nuptials, but never quite like that... as in totally unrecognizable.

"Since you vetoed all of the themes I presented as possibilities for the ceremony, Lorenzo suggested I perform it," Linde said, crossing her arms in an imperious stance.

Paige pushed away from the jamb. "You know what? Hilde hasn't picked out her music yet, but have you ever tried any other styles besides classical?" she asked. She knew that some pieces were less demanding than others, and the popularity of a song often made up for a poor performance.

"It's the bride's choice, of course," Paige said, making her stand clear. "But there are some less formal pieces that are traditional, too, that you might like."

With a smile of encouragement, Paige led Linde into the office, with its amazing sound system. Paige kept a selection of the most popular wedding songs on her phone, and she connected it to the computer.

"I have no interest in so-called modern music," Linde warned as she took her seat in a dramatic fashion.

"Why not?" Paige asked. "Why opera?"

"Because that's what Daddy would have wanted. My name and my destiny demand it," Linde answered loftily.

"I think you should choose your own destiny," Paige said while she glanced through the song listings.

"As the oldest, I feel I have to live up to Father's expectations," Linde said. But for once, Siegfried's sister didn't sound so sure of herself.

Paige turned to study her more closely. "Maybe he would just want you to be who you are," she said as sound filled the room.

Linde wrinkled her nose. She sat through a few of the usual showy arrangements of standards and some more modern pop tunes, but a quick shake of her head made her opinion clear. It wasn't until one of the mainstays of wedding receptions everywhere rang out that she showed any real interest.

"What's that?" she asked, leaning forward as the strains of "At Last" filled the room.

Paige smiled."That, Linde, is jazz."

CHAPTER SIXTEEN

By late afternoon, Linde had bought plenty of downloads to fuel her latest passion. To Paige, the change was music to her ears, not because she hated opera but because she hated the sound of Linde attempting to sing opera. And the most astonishing thing was that the girl's voice wasn't that bad.

When she wasn't trying to shriek out high notes she couldn't reach, but kept to a lower key, Linde's voice had a sultry quality that fit perfectly with her new style. Paige thought she might even be able to pull off "At Last" during the reception, with the band playing along.

As far as Paige was concerned, it was a win-win situation for everyone involved, except perhaps Lorenzo, an opera teacher without a pupil. But she had a suspicion the self-proclaimed maestro would manage to make himself indispensable in some other way.

The ensuing quiet was much more conducive to work, but Paige still couldn't concentrate. Going back to her accounts seemed like a chore, and snippets of the afternoon's songs popped into her head.

She sneaked peeks at the ocean and wondered if there was a way to access the strip of beach besides through the lab or down the abandoned path. Someone ought to put in a set of rustic wooden steps or at least some new flagstones.

Lost in thoughts of improving the grounds, Paige nearly jumped when she heard a masculine throat clearing. Her first thought was of Siegfried, and against all reasoning, her heart leapt in anticipation as she turned.

But draped in the doorway, with one arm casually braced against the jamb and a coat jacket slung over his shoulder, was a guy Paige had never seen before. Having grown accustomed to odd comings and goings around the estate, she wasn't alarmed.

In fact, what struck her most was how good-looking he was, with his chiseled cheekbones and dimpled chin. But the way he was posed, like a male model, seemed designed for maximum effect, which kind of negated the whole good-looking thing.

"Yes? May I help you?" Paige asked. Where was Godfrey? Wasn't he supposed to be doing something? Anything?

The guy flashed a grin that looked so practiced, it reminded Paige of Mia. "I just thought I'd check up on you," he said in a seductive tone.

Moving out of his pose, he stalked into the room as though he owned it, which made Paige even more curious about his identity. He definitely was a different sort than the other strange houseguests she'd met, but maybe he was an actor or, more likely, a wannabe.

Leaning forward, he held out a hand, as though to draw out the suspense of his introduction. And once assured of her complete attention, he flashed another smile.

"Blake Maitland," he said in a low voice that practically purred.

So this was Siegfried's cousin. Paige shook his hand readily enough, but he prolonged the contact until she was forced to slip her fingers from his.

"I was surprised to hear that Bebe had a new assistant, so I thought I'd come over and check you out," he said. The tilt of his lips suggested another meaning to his choice of words. "She's too dotty to keep anyone for long."

He tossed off the insult to his grandmother while eyeing Paige up and down in a way that made her stiffen. He was checking her out all right, and she didn't like it. Nor did she like the way he talked about Bebe.

"But now I'm *really* surprised," he said. "I expected one of those crazy New Agers she likes to pick up off the streets."

"I'm sorry to disappoint you," Paige said.

"Oh, I'm definitely not disappointed." Without an invitation, he dropped into the chair facing the desk.

"Well, that's a relief," Paige said dryly. "But I hardly would call Bebe dotty."

He smirked. "Oh, come on. She can't run this house. She's no longer involved in the company. It's only a matter of time..."

His words trailed off, and at that moment, Paige could see a resemblance to Siegfried. But the boy genius's eyes were full of wonder and openness, while Blake's were like the rest of his glossy presentation: all show and no substance.

"But let's not talk here," he said. He lifted his hand to his chin in a studied motion designed to focus attention on his handsome face and long, lean fingers. Paige was unimpressed.

"How about dinner tonight?" He named one of the city's most exclusive restaurants, and Paige recalled how she once had hoped Siegfried might take her there. But the place no longer held the same allure. However tempting the venue, the company was not.

"No, thanks," Paige said.

The stunned look that passed over Blake's face was so comical Paige nearly laughed. But he masked the emotion quickly, and she realized that's just what his attractive visage was: a mask.

No doubt he was used to women panting at the very sight of him, which accounted for his surprise at her refusal. Along with his looks, he probably worked his wealth and position so well that he had only to crook his finger—or strategically place it on his chin—and women came running.

"Do you know who I am?" he asked, his mouth curving seductively.

Paige smiled. She had him so figured out. His face having failed him, he was bringing up the wealth and power part.

"Yes. I believe you're Siegfried's cousin," Paige said.

Obviously, that was not the answer he wanted because he frowned momentarily before his mask slipped back into place once more. "I'm president of The Maitland Company," he said, lifting his dark brows.

When Paige eyed him expectantly, he shrugged. "Look, we

don't have to do that place. It's over-rated anyway. Tell me where you want to go," he said seductively.

"I'm really not interested in going anywhere."

He blew out a breath. "Hey, if you're on some kind of freak diet, just say so. I'm not into that whole raw food thing, but we could go see a show, theater, music, whatever."

"Opera?" Paige suggested.

He eyed her blankly.

"Just kidding," she said. "Thanks for the offer, but I'm not interested. Now, if you'll excuse me, I need to get back to work."

He leaned closer, not bothering to disguise his annoyance. "Hey, I don't know what you're angling for here," he began.

But Paige cut him off. "I'm just here to plan the wedding."

His dark brows drew together. "What?"

"I'm the wedding planner for Flosshilde and Mack. You do realize they're getting married?"

He shifted in his chair, all traces of the charmer gone as a suspicious expression marred his perfect features. "Are you a friend of theirs?"

"No," Paige said. "Bebe hired me."

"Then just what are you doing here?" he asked, gesturing to her opulent office. And for some reason, the question rankled, making her covet the space more than ever.

"Bebe asked me to arrange a couple other things for her," Paige said.

His face darkened. "Like a new heating system."

Paige nodded. She maintained a neutral tone even as she wondered just what was up with this guy. Did he expect her to get his approval first? As far as she knew, he had no control over Bebe, Siegfried, or anything about this house.

"Look, I bet you think you've got yourself a cozy spot here, but don't get too settled in. I have a vested interest in this family, and nobody messes with me."

"Excuse me?" Paige asked. "I'm just doing my job."

"Me too, babe. I'm the head of the family, and no one puts

one over on me," Blake said, rising to his feet and pointing a finger at her.

"I'm sorry. I thought Siegfried Maitland was the head of this family," Paige said. But she regretted her comment immediately. Making an enemy of Blake was not going to improve her business connections.

"You're right. I am the head of the family."

Blake turned at the sound, and Paige peeked around him to see Siegfried standing at the door. She grinned, filled with a ridiculous excitement. Siegfried was home, and she felt like running across the room and flinging herself into his arms. But would he catch her?

Blake straightened. "You're back," he said. "I hope the conference was productive."

Siegfried nodded, then glanced at Paige, who tried not to appear too giddy with pleasure at the sight of him. But for once, his own expression was not open, and she felt a sudden disappointment.

"Look, I don't know what Bebe's got going on here, Cuz, but you better keep an eye on things or your inheritance will be wiped out," Blake said, cocking a head in Paige's direction.

Paige swallowed a protest, while Siegfried stood in stony silence until his cousin finally moved toward the door.

"Well, you probably want to get back to the lab, so I'll catch you at the office," Blake said, reaching out to squeeze Siegfried's arm in a faux friendly fashion.

"I'll walk you out," Siegfried said.

Blake looked surprised but shrugged. "Sure, if you've got the time..." There was no mistaking his implication that Siegfried should be busy elsewhere. But he said nothing more as he followed his cousin from the room.

Watching them go, Paige was struck by the differences between them. They might share some genes and some looks, but there the similarities ended.

Blake was dressed in an expensive suit, and his every word and gesture screamed money, power, position—and vanity. Siegfried, on the other hand, easily could be mistaken for a penniless skateboarder. But he was the head of the family, the head of the company, and a genius inventor.

And no amount of dressing up or dressing down could hide who was the better man. No matter how handsome Blake thought himself, he was a selfish creep, while Siegfried was... Siegfried. A guy like no other.

CHAPTER SEVENTEEN

Since Blake Maitland hadn't seemed very pleased with her, Paige was surprised when his secretary called, asking her to stop by the company headquarters to discuss the wedding. Paige knew Blake wasn't involved in the ceremony, so she wondered what they had to talk about.

Still, she was all for mending fences, particularly for business purposes. The Maitland wedding was not an end in itself, but an opportunity. She needed other assignments, and Blake might just put the word out if he could be assured of her skills.

Swallowing her dislike of the man himself, Paige put on her most professional manner for her trip to The Maitland Company building. This time she had an easier pass through security, and she wondered whether Blake was responsible.

If so, he had more clout than Siegfried or Bebe, which was not a comforting thought. Paige stepped off the elevator warily, but her fears were eased by Ms. Feagin—Latasha—who let out a whoop of delight.

"Girl, you are a welcome sight, and I'm sure I'm not the only one who thinks so," the receptionist said slyly.

For some reason, Paige felt her face heat.

Latasha leaned forward and lowered her voice. "We're all glad to see the boss getting some of his own."

Paige wasn't sure quite what the woman meant by "getting," but she felt she ought to clarify her position. "I have an appointment with Blake," she said.

Latasha's dark brows shot upward.

"He wants to discuss the wedding."

The receptionist snorted with laughter. "Sure he does."

"What?" Paige asked, feeling a bit out of her depth. Was there some office politics going on that she didn't know about? If so, she better get informed fast. "What's up with the guy?"

Latasha smirked. "He's your boy's evil twin."

"What?"

"Okay, maybe they don't look enough alike to be twins, but Blake is bad news, just like his daddy was."

At Paige's blank look, Latasha motioned her closer. "You have to get with the program here! You've got to know the rules, if you're gonna be in the game."

Paige nodded, if still a bit blankly.

"Blake is the son of Bebe's younger boy, Raymond, who was quite the player in his day."

"He wasn't an inventor?"

Latasha laughed. "Uh, no. The only thing he invented was new ways to go through his inheritance. He called himself an entrepreneur, but he didn't work. He played. And he married."

"Who did he marry?"

"Who didn't he marry?" Latasha asked, with a laugh. "His first wife was Melissa Charles, an East Coast socialite whose money he enjoyed spending, usually on other women. When she grew tired of that, he married his lady of the moment, Darla, a Las Vegas showgirl. She's the mother of Blake and Mia."

"What?" Paige blinked. She had never sorted out the heiress's paternity, having been too busy disliking the girl. "But they have different last names."

"After he moved on, Darla married Buzzy Anderson, the sausage king. And Raymond took on ever younger wives until his heart attack, supposedly while cavorting with several expensive ladies, if you get my meaning. Mia, who was not exactly the grieving daughter, took her stepfather's name."

Paige's animosity toward the heiress faded with the realization that the lives of the rich and famous weren't always enviable. She could just picture young Mia being passed around from one jet-setter to another, with even less stability than Paige had growing up in apartments. At least Paige had a loving mother, a constant presence in her life.

"Poor Mia," Paige said.

Latasha appeared less sympathetic. "Maybe. I guess by the time Bebe got a hold of her, she was already pretty wild. She and her brother both seem to take after their daddy."

"But Blake must have more smarts than his father," Paige said, with a nod to the spacious offices of the president of The Maitland Company.

"Or maybe he has more ambition," Latasha said.

They both turned toward the glassed-in area that led to his private suite. The receptionist's tone did not make ambition sound like a good thing, and Paige was reminded of the arrogance she had encountered when she met the guy. She felt a certain wariness as she realized her plan to mend fences might be naïve. Instead, she'd be swimming with the sharks, or at least one of them, and she felt woefully unprepared.

She turned back to Latasha. "What do you suppose he wants with me?"

Latasha gave her a look. "If you can't figure that out, you are dumb *and* blind."

"Uh, he's a player?" Paige asked hesitantly. She wasn't model material, but the guy had invited her out the other day. Maybe he came on to every female he met, even non-runway types.

"Well, that too. But mainly, he's making trouble, as usual," Latasha said. "Family trouble."

When Paige looked blank again, Latasha rolled her eyes. "He's poaching on his cousin."

"What?" Paige felt a sudden panic. Was Blake going to try to ruin the wedding?

"You heard me. Blake is sniffing around you because he knows that Siegfried is interested."

"In me?" Paige said, her voice an un-businesslike squeak. "But that's impossible."

Latasha gave her a look that made Paige blush. Okay, so the boy genius had kissed her, and there had been the after-wedding make-out session. But then he had crawled back into his lab, never to be heard from again, which wasn't exactly the behavior of an interested guy.

Even when she'd put him to bed, he hadn't displayed awareness of her or anything else. And she hadn't seen him since, until the other day when Blake showed up.

"No way," Paige said, shaking her head.

Latasha's dark brows shot up. "Everyone's been talking since you first showed up here. I told you then that Siegfried doesn't get many visitors."

"Whatever interest he might have had is long gone," Paige said, surprised at the disappointment that came with the admission. But who could blame her for being a little hurt? After all, she was practically living in his home, and she never even caught a glimpse of him. "He's totally forgotten about me."

"Uh, no," Latasha said. "Word is that Blake was out to the house just recently and saw for himself what was going on."

"Nothing is going on," Paige protested. Siegfried wasn't even there when Blake arrived. Then the two of them had left together. Paige frowned. Had the boy genius said something?

Paige spent one delicious moment imagining Siegfried telling his cousin to back off his property, but the fantasy was so ludicrous that she couldn't hold onto it for long. Shaking her head, she met Latasha's skeptical gaze.

"I'm telling you that nothing went on. Blake came out to the estate and was questioning my right to be there when Siegfried appeared." To save the day. Or something.

Latasha lifted her dark brows again, and Paige stifled a groan. As flattering as her take on the situation was, Paige wasn't buying. Like Zoe, the receptionist was well intentioned but had no idea what she was talking about.

Siegfried was not interested. And neither was Blake, who was more likely to accuse her of pilfering the family silver from her cushy berth at the mansion. The thought was not comforting. She could just picture the burly security guys hauling her off, which might get Siegfried's attention.

Not that she wanted his attention, Paige reminded herself. As for Blake, he thought his grandmother was in her dotage, so maybe he was just looking out for his relatives. He couldn't be as bad as Latasha said, could he? Employees were often biased about their bosses.

So why couldn't Paige shake off a feeling of doom? She took a deep breath and turned toward the glassed-in area.

"Just say no," Latasha called after her.

Paige smiled, a genuine response that lasted until she was greeted by an even more gorgeous but less friendly face. Blake's assistant stalked across the plush carpet like she was the head supermodel, and Paige couldn't help wondering whether she pulled personal duty in order to rule the place. Or maybe intimate tasks were a perk. After all, Blake was rich, handsome, and powerful.

And his office reflected all those things. Although Paige wasn't impressed with much about him, she had to admit that the space was amazing. It was larger and even more luxurious than Siegfried's, which didn't seem quite right.

Wasn't Siegfried the head of the family and the company? She'd have to get with Latasha on the particulars. But maybe Blake conducted more business, she thought, vowing to keep an open mind.

And yet, when Blake flashed his white teeth in greeting, Paige was sharply reminded of a shark. And as he came around the desk to shake her hand, she briefly wondered if he might bite it off.

Worse, he covered their joined hands with his left in an intimate gesture that made her uncomfortable. Forced to slip her fingers from his, Paige made for the nearest chair, hoping he'd return to his spot behind the desk, putting the furniture between them.

But he perched on the corner of the massive piece in a pose that might have been taken from a men's magazine. Did the guy practice this stuff in the mirror? Paige had to choke back an inappropriate laugh.

Although she'd seen similar types in bars and clubs, rich jerks looking for a hookup, Blake was playing on a whole other level. Really wealthy guys like him probably went to Cannes or Paris runway shows to troll for dates.

Or not. From the way he was looking at her, Paige had the distinct feeling he was trolling her way. She cleared her throat.

"Lovely office," she said.

Blake shrugged, as if the amenities were of no consequence to him. "It makes the company look good, which is vital. A successful business needs the proper image, as I'm sure you know."

Paige nodded politely, although she wondered if the comment was some sort of dig at Siegfried, who certainly wouldn't fit any slick presentations. The boy genius did not look at home in his space the way Blake did. Nor was he a people person, the kind who could wheel and deal in the corporate world. Blake, on the other hand, probably could embezzle half the company with one hand tied behind his back and a smile on his face.

He certainly was giving her the business right now, oozing charm as he leaned close. "Now, tell me just what you're doing for my lovely young cousin and her fiancé."

So Paige told him, briefly sketching the wedding plans. Since he was a member of the family, she felt comfortable discussing the general arrangements, but he didn't appear very interested. In fact, he soon turned the conversation back to himself.

"Look, I'm sorry if I came on a bit too strong the other day," he said.

"No problem," Paige said, relieved that he seemed to have dismissed his suspicions about her.

"I guess I'm guilty of being a little overprotective of my family," he said softly, as if sharing a confidence.

"Well, that's understandable," Paige murmured. Hey, if that's the spin he wanted to put on it, fine. But Paige knew better. She saw more of his family than he did, and she knew that no one was looking out for them.

Fences mended, as her mom would say, Paige was ready to go. But Blake wasn't finished, as she found out when he put a hand atop her own. Again.

Uh-oh. Maybe she was a little slow to catch on, but who could blame her? Not exactly the gorgeous model type, Paige never had to fend off guys, even in bars. Although she had been hit on before, it was never with such practiced skill or determination.

It was baffling. She was probably the least attractive woman in the building, barring any unseen cafeteria help or cleaning crews.

Slipping her fingers from his once more, Paige cleared her throat. It was time to make a graceful exit.

"Well, Mr. Maitland," Paige began.

"Blake," he interrupted, flashing his white teeth.

"All right. Blake," she said. "If you have any further questions about the wedding, just give me a call. But right now, I really must get going."

"Yes, let's go to lunch," he said, his voice a low purr.

"Uh, no," Paige said, rising to her feet.

"All right," Blake said as he, too, stood. "Tonight then. When you have dinner with me, we can move on to more interesting subjects."

Paige could just imagine what those would be: Blake, Blake, and more Blake. The topic might fascinate his assistant, who was getting paid to listen, but it would bore her to tears. "No, thank you."

He had stepped toward her, to put a proprietary hand on her back, and now he leaned in, so his face was uncomfortably close to hers. "Too short notice? How about later in the week?"

Paige sought an answer that was more diplomatic than the truth of the matter, which was that she didn't want anything to do with him. She smiled tightly. "I'm afraid that won't be possible. I don't mix business with my personal life."

His mask slipped for a second as his voice rose. "Really? That's interesting because from what I hear, Siegfried's been trailing after you like a lost pup."

Paige stiffened. "Well, you must be mistaken."

Mask back in place, he assumed a more casual tone. "Hey, let's be honest here. Siegfried is a nice guy. We all appreciate what he does for the company," he said, making it sound as though his cousin did no more than wash the windows.

"But he has some form of ADD, a hyper focus or something. He has his mind on his work, and he doesn't pay attention to anything else. And that includes women."

Paige wondered just how Siegfried could follow her around like a pup if he were hyper focused on his work, but she said nothing. She simply walked toward the door.

"His father didn't believe in medications. He said there was no stifling genius. Courting mediocrity and all that," Blake said.

Paige had to bite her lip. She wanted to tell this slick player that he ought to know plenty about being mediocre. And being a user. If Blake had his way, the boy genius probably would be chained to his desk.

Her hand on the latch, Paige turned to say goodbye, but Blake caught up with her, his expression hard. "Hey, if you think you're going to get something out of this family, you can forget it right now," he warned.

"Oh, I intend to get something all right," Paige said, and she had the pleasure of seeing Blake's mouth twist into a frown. "I intend to get the satisfaction that comes from putting on a great wedding."

Flashing her own teeth, Paige made her exit, leaving Blake Maitland standing alone, looking furious.

So much for mending fences.

CHAPTER EIGHTEEN

Siegfried couldn't focus.

More accurately, he couldn't focus on his work, which had never happened to him before. It was such an unusual affliction that he'd come to the company's lab, hoping that getting with his team might help. But so far he was no better off than at the house. And at least there he had a chance of seeing her.

But she was the problem.

Ever since he'd come back from the conference, he'd felt queasy—like he did when he failed to eat and sleep. But he couldn't think of that without remembering the night she'd put him to bed. Or had that all been a dream?

He couldn't be sure since finding her with Blake. Not that she was actually doing anything with his cousin. But the subtle cues of human behavior often escaped him. And Blake's exploits with women were well known. Even down in the lab, Siegfried had heard rumors about the number of killer rich girls, models, and high-priced hookers Blake ran through.

In fact, Bebe was always bemoaning her other grandson's behavior and holding Siegfried up as an example of proper conduct. As if Blake were going to emulate him.

Blake didn't. In fact, the two had never had anything in common. From birth, Blake had been the wild kid, driving expensive cars without a license and trying all manner of mind-numbing chemicals, while Siegfried had been happily tucked away in the lab with his father. A born geek.

Even after the death of his parents, Siegfried never moved in the same circles as his cousin. He'd been sent off early to college, so it wasn't until Blake was named president of the company that they came into anything except sporadic contact.

Over the past few years, Blake had made some overtures, but Siegfried had learned to keep his distance. He let Blake run the business end of things, while he did his research, and they rarely saw each other beyond the boardroom.

Blake wasn't close to his sister, so he never came out to the house even though Mia lived there now. And he avoided his disapproving grandmother like the plague.

So when Siegfried had returned home from his conference to find Blake hanging out in the estate's office with Paige, he had been stunned. He'd stood there, uncomprehending, as though someone had snuck into his lab and lifted his work when he wasn't looking.

But Paige wasn't work. And she sure wasn't his, despite the times he'd managed to connect with her. As usual, he'd made a muddle of things. Even he knew that someone that beautiful and amazing couldn't be expected to wait around for him. Hadn't he promised himself to stay focused on her?

Instead, he had gone back to robotics and gotten too involved in it. He felt like he was on the verge of a breakthrough and just wanted to keep going until he found the answer. But, like he often did, he ended up burning out, instead.

Usually, after a few days of overwork, he would have woken up, facedown on the keyboard, drooling into the circuitry. But this time, it was different. This time, he had been totally immersed in what he was doing when he had heard a voice calling him. Her voice.

At first, he thought he was hallucinating. But when he turned, she was there, like a hologram. Only real. Alive and breathing and Paige.

But by then he was too fried to do anything except shove in some food and fall into bed. And when he woke up a day later, he barely remembered any of it, just that moment when he turned and saw her there beside him. He was convinced he had dreamed the whole thing until Godfrey asked him if Ms. Porter had given him a good washing.

Unfortunately, Siegfried was certain there had been no bathing involved. But, still, he knew he had blown it again. He'd actually had her in his bedroom, and he'd been too exhausted to do anything except collapse onto the mattress.

And had he done anything since? No. He had gone to his conference and wondered what to do next. And then... it was too late.

Siegfried was so lost in thought that he nearly jumped when Takeo nudged him. The team member wore such a funny look that Siegfried immediately paid attention. Had Takeo found some problem in their latest working model? But the guy only pointed toward where their third team member, Kevin, stood holding the lab phone.

"Dude, you have a girlfriend?" Kevin asked.

What? Siegfried felt a twinge of panic. Had he been speaking his thoughts aloud? He'd been warned not to do so for security purposes, but sometimes he still mumbled.

"Dude!" Kevin said when Siegfried didn't respond. "Latasha from reception is on the phone, and she says your woman is up there."

"What?" Siegfried felt his twinge of panic combine with queasiness to form a cocktail of suspicion. Was this another one of Blake's nasty jokes?

"According to Latasha, she just went into Blake's office, so you might want to drop by and grab her for lunch or something."

Siegfried froze. Blake's office? He'd always let his cousin do whatever with the company, but now he felt an overwhelming urge to go up there and throw the bastard out. Or something.

Kevin held out the phone. "Do you want to talk to Latasha?"

Siegfried shook his head even as he tried to picture the girl in reception. He didn't have a good memory for faces, and as his sudden anger cooled, he realized the whole thing probably was some prank set up by Blake.

But what if it wasn't?

"What should I tell her?" Kevin asked.

Siegfried lurched to his feet. "I'll be right up."

As he made his way to the elevator, Siegfried told himself that his days of being the butt of older kids' jokes were over.

He was an adult, and so was everyone in this office, although that hadn't stopped Blake from messing with him.

"Dude, who is this chick?" Kevin asked, moving toward him. Takeo was not far behind, wide-eyed. Siegfried shook his head. Was it any wonder he hadn't asked these guys for advice about women? They were even more clueless than he was.

"You said she was the receptionist," Siegfried said. Or was she Blake's assistant? He hoped not.

"Not her, although the receptionist is pretty hot," Kevin said. "Who's the chick she's talking about, the one she called your woman?"

Siegfried sought to avoid the question by stepping into the elevator, but his team joined him there.

"I wish to see the woman of yours," Takeo explained when Siegfried shot him a look.

"She's not my woman. There is no such woman," Siegfried said.

"Then why are you going up there?" Kevin asked.

"Just to see what's going on," Siegfried said. He thought quickly. "She might be referring to the wedding planner. There must be some confusion about why I need to see her."

"Why do you need to see her?" Kevin asked.

"You are getting married?" Takeo said.

"No!" Siegfried said. He was starting to sweat. "My sister is."

"What does that have to do with you, dude?"

"I'm the one paying for it," Siegfried said.

"So?"

"So, you guys better get back to work," Siegfried said. He stepped out of the elevator and scanned the lobby. There was no sign of Paige. He glanced at the receptionist, who tilted her head toward Blake's domain.

Now what? He couldn't exactly barge in there. Then Blake would really know something was up. And what was Paige doing there, anyway? She probably wanted to see Blake, that's what, he thought queasily.

"If she's in with Blake, you'll never see her again," Kevin said, echoing Siegfried's worst fears. Still, Siegfried started forward until Kevin grabbed his arm.

"Dude! Watch out for Lisa," Kevin said, pointing to Blake's assistant, seated inside her glass throne room.

Her name wasn't really Lisa, but Kevin likened her to a famously scary video game character. She was some kind of Amazon who looked down on everyone in the company, even Siegfried. And she guarded Blake like a mad dog.

"Siegfried is CEO. He can get by her," Takeo said.

Siegfried wasn't so sure. Thankfully, he didn't have to find out because Paige stepped from Blake's office at that exact moment, and Siegfried could only stare. He'd forgotten how great she looked.

"Hey, dude. She's hot," Kevin said. Every female Kevin ever saw was hot, but this time Siegfried felt like agreeing.

For good or ill, she was heading right toward them, so Siegfried braced himself for the usual awkwardness. But the closer she got, the better he felt, until he just wanted to pull her into his arms.

How could he ever have let himself become distracted by work? He wished he could drag her back to his bedroom now and keep here there. Forever.

"Siegfried!" When she finally saw him, there was no mistaking the pleasure that lit her face, though she hung back. As always, Siegfried tried to guess what that meant and came up wanting.

"Hey," Kevin said, reminding Siegfried that he and Takeo were watching. He introduced them, and Paige shook hands with each of them in turn. Siegfried wanted to take his turn, too, holding her hand, holding her...

"You are Siegfried's woman?" Takeo said.

The question hung in the air, like that moment when the weight of the rider, the force of gravity, and the forces of the ground pushing up on the skateboard all balanced out to zero. Paige visibly faltered.

"Sorry," Siegfried said. "He doesn't have a great grasp of

English."

"This is not his woman?" Takeo asked Kevin, looking confused.

"Dude, he said she was the wedding planner. Remember?" Kevin said, but he was staring at Paige as though he'd never shaken hands with a female before. Maybe he hadn't.

Siegfried stepped forward. "We were just breaking for lunch, and I thought you might like to go eat something. Since you're here."

It sounded lame, even to his ears, and he wished their audience, the offices, and everything else would disappear. He was at his best when it was just the two of them. Outside. In the dark.

"Oh! I'd love to, but I have an appointment." She sounded sincere, and yet Siegfried wasn't good at reading people.

"But it was nice meeting you all," she added, nodding toward his coworkers. She wasn't looking him in the eye, which Siegfried knew wasn't good.

He watched her step into the elevator and fought an urge to seize her and drag her back. To his office. To his lab. Anywhere. But what could he do?

"Maybe I'll see you at the house, then?" he asked, finally managing to say something. Anything.

"If you come out of the lab," she said, with a smile. And then she was gone.

For a moment Siegfried just stood there staring after her, something clenching in his chest. He took a deep breath and tried to think, to examine the situation logically.

But sometimes, other members of his team could see the problem more clearly than he did. And beside him, Kevin shook his head.

"Dude," he said. "You need to stop working so much."

The bleak silence that followed as that truth sunk in was broken by Takeo, who wore an expression of bafflement. "I do not understand. Is that your woman or not?"

"Not," Siegfried said.

"So she is the woman of Blake?"

"No!" Siegfried said. At least, he hoped not. That was the big question, wasn't it? How much good would it do to curtail his projects if Blake was making his time? Or the time he would like to make?

"I do not understand. Why are we here?" Takeo said.

Good question.

"Maybe we should ask her," Kevin said. They all turned to Latasha, who was inclining her head toward Siegfried as if to call him over.

"She scares me," Takeo said, blinking.

"They all scare me," Kevin said.

Siegfried glanced around the offices and realized Paige was right. The women were kind of intimidating looking, at least to guys like him and his team. He'd never really noticed before because he rarely talked to any of them.

Until now. Latasha was gesturing more forcefully, so he had no choice but to walk over to her huge round desk, the hub of the floor that housed the top executives.

"Well?" she asked, without preamble.

"Uh, she had to go," Siegfried said, hoping he wasn't expected to explain in more detail. His team hung back, within earshot, and he really didn't want to get into the whole "your woman" thing again with the receptionist as they listened.

Obviously, the phrase had been wishful thinking on Kevin's part, coupled with the confusion of someone who only occasionally interacted with other humans. Again, Siegfried was reminded why he'd never gone to those two for advice about Paige.

Rather than ask why she'd called the lab in the first place, Siegfried took the opportunity to discover the reason Paige had been here. With Blake. He leaned closer and lowered his voice. "Do you know why she was in the building?"

Latasha leaned in and rolled her eyes. "Mr. Maitland wanted to talk to her about the wedding."

"Why?" As far as Siegfried knew, Blake had nothing to do with his relatives, let alone plans for an event he wasn't even likely to attend.

Latasha lifted her brows, as though the answer were obvious. "Honey, that boy wants whatever you've got."

It took a moment for Siegfried to realize "that boy" referred to the president of the company, and the rest of the statement was even more puzzling. "But I don't have anything he wants."

Latasha's brows lifted even higher. "Don't you?"

Siegfried stared at her numbly, unable to comprehend what she was saying. No wonder Kevin had been confused by the phone call.

Siegfried glanced toward his cousin's office, certain of only one thing. Blake had always been better-looking, more popular, and able to charm any woman. So if he wanted Paige...

As though reading his thoughts, Latasha made a dismissive sound. "Your Paige is too smart to fall for that one," she said. But then one of the phone lines rang, and she turned away to speak into her headset.

Siegfried didn't know whether to be relieved or disappointed by the abrupt end of the conversation. He walked back to where his team waited, eyeing him expectantly, and groaned.

He'd always traveled under the radar, keeping his head down and his mind on his work. So why was it that suddenly everyone from his driver to the office personnel knew more about his private life than he did?

"*What?*" Zoe's shriek pierced the quiet of the Rose Garden at Golden Gate Park, but thankfully the clients had already left, so no one was disturbed except a few nearby birds. And Paige.

"Now, let me get this straight," Zoe said."You've practically moved into the Maitland mansion, and now you have both rich, successful cousins after you?"

"I have not practically moved into the Maitland mansion," Paige said, taking a deep breath of the fragrant air. She'd put off telling her assistant about the office for this very reason.

"Bebe Maitland, one of the scions of San Francisco, gives you space in her landmark house, and you haven't moved in?

Why not?" Zoe demanded. "Come on, Cinderella, get with the script!"

Paige laughed. "Bebe Maitland is not my fairy godmother."

"Oh really?" Zoe asked. "Because it sure seems to me like she waved her wand and transformed your life from peon to princess."

Paige shot her a look. "I am not a peon."

"Although technically you aren't sleeping among the cinders, that apartment of yours is pretty tiny."

But it's mine, not someone else's, Paige thought. Unlike Zoe, she refused to depend on anyone except herself. And she did not like owing people, no matter how free they were with their largesse.

"I'm doing my part in return, working as sort of an unpaid assistant since she has trouble keeping employees," Paige said. "So there's no transformation involved. I'm not being outfitted for a ball gown or driven around in a coach."

"No, you have access to a fleet of coaches and your own driver!" Zoe said. "And it doesn't matter if you've got a glass slipper as long as the prince puts a ring on it."

"I don't believe in fairy tales or princes," Paige said. She'd never bought into that fantasy even as a child. And if her mother's broken dreams hadn't been all the evidence she needed, her job proved that even the most romantic wedding did not ensure the future of any couple.

"Quit focusing on the details and just go with it! So maybe he doesn't ride a white charger, just a skateboard," Zoe said with a shrug. "That doesn't make him any less of a prince."

Paige smiled at that image of Siegfried Maitland coming to anyone's rescue, except maybe a robot with bad programming. Instead of scooping her up to carry her off into the sunset, the boy genius had knocked her down. And then forgotten about her.

Paige's silence did not deter her friend. "This is a once-in-a-lifetime opportunity!" Zoe said. "You need to seize the dream and ride it to your own happy ending!"

"Have you been overdosing on animation?" Paige asked,

dismissing all thoughts of riding anything, including a skateboard built for two.

"I already have a dream, thanks, and it's a thriving business," Paige said. "And I don't plan on giving it up for the dubious privilege of organizing someone else's schedule, without pay or benefits, no matter how nice the surroundings."

Zoe opened her mouth to argue, but Paige shook her head. She was enjoying her luxurious office, and she would continue to take advantage of the opportunities Bebe provided. But there was no point in getting attached to anything—or anyone—at the Maitland mansion.

"This is not a position that boasts a good track record," Paige explained. "Sooner or later, I'll get kicked to the curb, probably by Blake Maitland." And probably sooner than later.

Zoe frowned. "Yeah, as much as I'm all for rich, handsome movers and shakers, I don't know about Blake Maitland. He's got kind of a reputation."

"As a player?" Paige asked, remembering what Latasha had told her.

"As a jerk," Zoe said.

CHAPTER NINETEEN

For the next few weeks Paige was busy with other clients and stayed away from her luxury office, eager to avoid any more run-ins with Blake. She wouldn't mind giving up her space, but she sure didn't want to be fired. Thankfully, all was quiet from that quarter, so she began to relax.

But Blake wasn't the only problem Maitland.

When wedding business forced Paige finally to drive out to the house, she found that Hilde had blown her off again. Even the slow-moving Godfrey took one look at her face and exited rapidly after giving her the news.

Paige was tempted to follow him. In fact, she was tempted to march over to the garages and break down the doors to Hilde's apartments. And then she just might drag out the world's most elusive client and her invisible fiancé. If he even existed. Paige was beginning to wonder whether the prospective marriage was a joke perpetrated by Bebe Maitland so she and her houseguests could gain access to someone with organizational skills, an unpaid, communal secretary of sorts.

Okay, so maybe even the overzealous Tad would draw the line at that conspiracy theory. But there was no denying that the Maitland-Johnson nuptials were the weirdest Paige had ever encountered. And that included the reality TV shows she refused to watch.

Because of the bride's lack of interest, the events had been kept to a minimum. There were no golf outings, no showers that Paige knew about, no pre- or after-parties. Hilde had even refused a rehearsal dinner, which was a first for Paige.

It was just the bare bones: a wedding and reception. And that would be enough for Paige to make her name—if she could keep them on track. But for once in her life she was behind. And although she charged the Maitland account for all the useless trips she made and wasted time she spent chasing down those involved, what good was the money without her showcase? Her future depended on this success.

But Hilde seemed determined to sabotage her own celebration. She was the queen of procrastination and indecision, a bane of planners everywhere. Paige wasn't sure whether this behavior was typical of the girl or if there was something more sinister behind her evasiveness.

And by sinister, she meant the mysterious Mack Johnson, a painter no one had ever heard of and Paige had never seen. This was the only time in her career that she hadn't held her initial meeting with both members of the bridal couple, and she still hadn't laid eyes on the groom.

It wasn't just his furtive behavior that bothered Paige. She couldn't understand the dearth of information on a guy who was marrying into a wealthy and influential family that might or might not be involved in secret government contracts. Tad ought to be on that case, instead of on hers.

And yet, no one in the Wackyland of the mansion seemed to harbor the slightest suspicion about the mystery man. As one of the few sane members of the household, Paige had taken it upon herself to perform an online search for Mack's name.

She'd found nothing, which raised even more red flags as far as she was concerned. But she had stopped short of having him investigated. Although acting as Bebe's unpaid assistant, she didn't want to overstep her boundaries.

Plus, she could end up cutting off her nose to spite her face, as her mom would say. Because if the wedding were called off, she wouldn't be able to pull it off. And that would be the end of her big opportunity to impress the city's elite with her skills.

Taking a deep breath, Paige vowed to do whatever was necessary to get the events back on schedule: arm-twisting, blackmail, sexual favors... Alone in the elegant office, she stifled a laugh at the thought of seducing anyone involved.

Although Siegfried immediately came to mind, he was too elusive to track down and didn't have the attention span required. Besides, seducing him would not produce the desired results, she told herself. But then Paige began to consider just what results would be produced, and only the sound of footsteps made her snap out of it.

Even then, she couldn't quite dismiss Good-looking Guy from her mind. Against all reason, she hoped he was the one knocking on the open door, though he was never around the mansion—or at least where she could see him.

Still, her heart began pounding just as loudly as the raps on the wood, for who else would be banging away when she was right within view? Only someone with poor social skills, she thought, turning with a smile.

It faded fast at the sight of the figure poised at the entrance—and still thumping with a delicate fist. Mia Anderson, spoiled heiress, was leaning against the frame, wearing her usual smirk. "Hello?"

Paige put on her best 'difficult client' expression. "Hello, Mia. I'm right here. You don't have to knock."

The heiress assumed a sulky look. "Well, Bebe gave us all a little lecture about respecting your privacy—even though you are a total freeloader."

And Mia wasn't? But Paige held her tongue.

"I'd like to fly to St. Barts as soon as you can arrange it," the heiress said.

Paige thought she was used to the weird requests tendered by Bebe's houseguests, but even she blinked in surprise. "Excuse me?"

"Aren't you the little errand girl?"

"Uh, no," Paige said. And if this was what came with the office, she would vacate. "I've been organizing Bebe's schedule," she began to explain, but Mia cut her off.

"And everyone else's, too," the heiress said.

"I've been lending a hand with appointments and whatnot," Paige said hedging. "If you don't want to make reservations yourself online, just call an agency."

Mia scowled. "You know the parents have cut me off, and Bebe throws her money away on strays," she said, with a pointed look at Paige.

Bebe was definitely not throwing money Paige's way, but she refused to get into that conversation. She was too puzzled by Mia's request. "Then how are you intending to pay for the tickets?"

"Don't you have miles or something?"

The ludicrousness of the wealthy heiress asking Paige to foot the bill for a luxury trip was too much. She would have burst into hysterical laughter if not for Mia's mutinous expression.

"Sorry," Paige said. "I don't have enough miles to visit my mother, let alone anywhere farther. And I work really hard for what I have." Which begged the question of why Mia didn't have a cushy position that required little besides her high profile. And by 'position,' Paige was not thinking of a sex tape.

"What about you? Wouldn't you like a job, with your own paycheck?" she asked.

"Doing what?" Mia said with a snort. "I can't get a reality contract, even low-budget cable, all by myself."

Paige tried not to wince at the thought of that freak show. "No. I mean a real job with the family business." Whatever that was.

Mia gaped at her as though she were speaking in tongues.

"You know. Downtown. The Maitland Company."

Mia snorted again. "Like Blake would let me."

It was Paige's turn to snort. "Blake Maitland is not the head of this family. Nor is he the head of the company." Paige felt her temper rise at the truth that everyone else seemed to forget. "Siegfried is."

Mia opened her mouth and shut it again, a definite first.

"You're an enterprising girl," Paige said. "You just need some business clothes, and you'll look even better than the rest of the supermodel staff."

Mia rolled her eyes, and Paige couldn't decide whether she was mocking work wear or the idea that any model could compete with her.

"I'd need something to do besides look good," she said. "Or I'd be bored there, too."

Paige gaped in shock but swallowed any objections or questions about qualifications. For all she knew, Mia might have a degree or a talent for... something besides smirking. "Well, then, ask Siegfried."

Mia's eyes narrowed, and Paige just knew she wasn't going to like what was coming next.

"How about *you* ask Siegfried?"

CHAPTER TWENTY

Paige let her head fall with a thud onto the immaculate surface of the desk. What had she been thinking?

She'd been thinking to get rid of Mia, no matter what she had to agree to in order to do it. But now, she would be forced to ask a favor of the boy genius.

If she could find him.

The memory of his bedroom and its exact location in the house came to her abruptly. But Siegfried would hardly be there in the afternoon unless he was sleeping off another marathon work session, and if so, he would be useless.

Still, the notion of checking that big bed for Tall, Dark, and Tousled was tempting. The prospect of looking in the lab was less so. She had no idea what the overzealous Tad might do if his boss weren't there to keep him in check. And she didn't want to know.

But the thought of driving back into the city a few minutes after arriving here wasn't appealing, either. If only she could call him, like a normal person, she thought wistfully. Maybe they could get the guy an old-school beeper or dog tags with GPS capabilities?

Paige was just getting ready to call Latasha to see if she knew whether he was at the office when she heard a discreet knock at the door. Again, she couldn't help but hope that her actions had conjured him up, and she would turn to find Siegfried slumping against the doorjamb sadly in need of a haircut and some decent clothes.

But, again, she was disappointed. Bebe stood in the opening, though she was far more welcome than most visitors. In fact, the matriarch might be able to do something about her elusive granddaughter and the mysterious Mack. Or find Mia gainful employment.

But before Paige could ask for help, Bebe stepped in. "I'm

so glad you're here," she said in that breathless way of hers.

Paige struggled to keep the smile on her face. What now? she thought dismally. Had the air-conditioning broken? Had the new gardener quit? Were there leaks in the elderly roof, which Paige had been meaning to look at? "Is there a problem?" she asked warily.

"Oh no, dear," Bebe said.

"Good," Paige said, breathing a sigh of relief. "Because I already have one. I was supposed to meet with Hilde, but she's not here."

"Oh, I'm sure she'll turn up eventually," Bebe said. She waved one hand in an airy gesture of dismissal, which was fine for someone with access to billions, but not fine for a wedding planner with a schedule to keep.

Paige was about to launch into her update on the poor progress of preparations, but Bebe waved a hand again, effectively silencing her. If only the matriarch could work such magic on her grandchildren, Paige thought. Or the wedding of the year.

"But there is something you can do right now in your position as the event planner," Bebe said.

Paige straightened up. Was there something she'd forgotten? Impossible. More likely, some relative or stranger had been left off the guest list. "Yes?"

"The dancing," Bebe said.

"The dancing?" Paige echoed. A live band, more like an orchestra to her way of thinking, had been engaged to play pop hits and standards, and Linde would sing some jazzier pieces, providing plenty of opportunities for the guests to move around the floor that would be set up outside.

"Well, not everyone knows how to dance," Bebe said.

Paige frowned. "But I'm sure Hilde told me she and Mack didn't want professional instruction."

While some couples were adamant that the traditional first, father-daughter, and mother-son turns be picture perfect, just as many others only wanted to have a good time. Paige couldn't imagine the looser atmosphere prevailing at such a high-end function, so maybe Bebe had convinced Hilde that lessons were required.

"Oh no," the older woman said, as if reading Paige's mind. "I'm not talking about the bride and groom. It's Siegfried who concerns me."

Yes, he concerns me, too, Paige thought. *But it's the bridal couple we need to focus on.* If Bebe spent more time concentrating on them, and not the boy genius, maybe the wedding of the year could get back on track.

"Well, I can try to schedule an appointment with an instructor, but your grandson is notoriously hard to pin down." Or locate. Or communicate with.

"Oh, he's here now," Bebe said. "I'll just have Godfrey fetch him."

Paige kept a firm grip on the jaw that threatened to drop open at the thought that Siegfried was nearby—and was expecting lessons immediately.

"That's awfully short notice," Paige said. "But I'll call a couple of my contacts and see what I can manage."

She kept her voice pleasant, even though she knew that by the time someone drove all the way out here, the student would be long gone. Into the lab. Onto the skateboard. Down the rabbit hole.

"Oh no, dear," Bebe said. "There's no point in going to all that trouble. I'm sure you can take care of it." She waved her fingers again, and Paige wondered if the woman should carry a wand—the better to get others to do her bidding.

"Take care of it?" Paige asked.

"Siegfried," Bebe said. "I'm sure you are experienced enough to teach him."

Paige froze as a myriad of thoughts flashed through her mind, both tantalizing and mortifying. For once, she was struck speechless and barely hung on to her professional demeanor.

"After all, you know the songs that will be used, and you have the music," Bebe said. "Just make sure he will do well enough not to cause a spectacle, not that Hilde and Mack would care, but Siegfried feels an obligation to the family. And there are some who are all too quick to criticize."

Paige knew the matriarch was talking about Blake and Mia, but she still couldn't get her head around the fact that Bebe Maitland expected her to get up close and personal with the boy genius.

"But I'm not..." Paige began, only to watch Bebe wave away any objections and make her exit, leaving the wedding planner to complete the sentence. "...a professional." Or ready. Or willing.

Not knowing how long it would take for Siegfried to appear—if he showed at all—Paige tried to compose herself. Although she'd never taught anyone, she knew what she was doing. She'd learned how to dance, just like she'd learned everything else to do with receptions. Because it was her job.

She'd never had to step in, so to speak, because who wants the wedding planner waltzing with the groom? But Siegfried wasn't the groom. And this was the wedding of the year, the event that would ensure her success. So she needed to put on her big-girl panties and just do it.

It might be easier if her student wasn't the best kisser she'd ever known and the memory of his talented hands on her eager body wasn't fresh in her mind. Way too fresh.

Blowing out a breath, Paige swiveled toward the computer and focused on business. She decided to give the man paying for this wedding a progress update, but when she opened her Maitland database the first thing that popped up was not a nuptial-related task.

Instead, she saw that the most prominent and pressing note was to get Mia a job.

Paige frowned. As onerous as that chore would be, at least it would take her mind off Tall, Dark, and Tousled. So she tried to come up with a good reason for hiring an empty-headed mean girl with no qualifications except a smirk and an acid tongue.

By the time Siegfried arrived, she'd managed to get herself back into professional mode. He was just a client, Paige told herself, although usually the kind of professionals whose clients felt them up were in a different sort of business.

But when he appeared, so handsome and seemingly glad to see her, Paige felt her unease disappear. She was glad to see him, too, even though she wouldn't admit it to anyone, especially not Zoe.

"I guess you're supposed to keep me from embarrassing myself," he said. His rueful smile kicked all of Paige's protective instincts into high gear. If she could get this guy to outshine his not-so-nice relatives, she'd be happy to do it for free.

"Since you are the head of one of the wealthiest and most connected families in the city and smarter than anyone else in any room, I don't think you should ever be embarrassed," Paige said. "Leave that to the rest of the populace."

He grinned, and her heart stopped. How did he do that to her? For a moment, she just stood there gaping at him, before coming to her senses.

"Uh, speaking of your family," she said awkwardly, "Mia wanted me to ask you something."

His expression turned wary, and why not? Paige was wary of Mia, too. And this errand. She took a deep breath. "She was hoping you might give her a job with the company, so she could earn her own money and gain some independence, and maybe, maturity."

Paige had prepared a speech about family and duty and second chances. And when Siegfried didn't turn green or flee the premises, she was about to launch into it. But he stopped her with a nod.

"Okay."

Paige gaped again. "Seriously? Doing what?"

He shrugged. "I don't know. I'll ask Willow."

Paige tossed out her lecture but added a caveat. "From what I was told, Blake probably won't like it."

"Good," Siegfried said. He grinned again, in a conspiratorial way, and Paige nearly shivered. Or was she too hot? It was suddenly warm in the room, and she went to the window to let in the ocean breeze.

"Nice," he said.

Was he talking about the office? The view? Her? Paige didn't speak his language, so she didn't know. Maybe there was an app for that? She was even more confused when he stepped closer. And closer.

For one crazy moment, she thought he was going to kiss her. It wasn't like he hadn't before. Or held her close. Or gotten personal with her undergarments. But then she realized the real reason he was here and cleared her throat.

"Let's start with a simple waltz," she said.

For all his seeming gawkiness, the guy wasn't uncoordinated. That much was evident from his skateboarding skills, as well as his self-proclaimed manual dexterity, though Paige faltered when she remembered the details of that demonstration.

"One. Two. Three. One, two, three." The box step was easily mastered, and the formal hold kept things from getting too intimate. They practiced turns and moving with the music, and Paige was surprised at how easily they fell into sync. In fact, it seemed as if they'd been doing this forever.

Although Paige viewed the ritual as cynically as everything else to do with weddings, she found herself drifting into a kind of dreamlike state. The lyrics to "I Could Have Danced All Night" suddenly made sense. Even without the twinkling lights or champagne or any of the trappings, Paige felt like they could go on forever.

Maybe the whole thing was a form of hypnotism. Because even when the song faded, Siegfried slowed his steps, and their formal hold dipped and fell away, Paige couldn't shake the sensation of bliss.

Was this how it happened? she wondered, with a twinge of panic. The romance and sweeping melodies and balmy breezes sucked you into the fairy tale, and the next thing you knew, you were a starry-eyed bride.

But Paige wasn't starry-eyed. She was smart enough to know that at some point the music stops and there's nothing left but real life and division of community property. Yet, even knowing all that, she felt herself swaying toward her partner, her resolve slipping away.

She found her voice with difficulty. "Uh, I think that's fine. For now."

When Siegfried reached for her, Paige stepped back, with even greater difficulty. She couldn't look him in the eyes, fearful of what she would see there—and even more fearful of what he might see in her own.

Zoe would say she was over-thinking it all, making too much of what could be a fun hookup with a good-looking guy. But Zoe was an incurable romantic who couldn't possibly envision the inevitable demise of a love affair or even the end of a fun hookup.

Unfortunately, Paige could picture it all too well, and she didn't want bad feelings or awkwardness resulting in a change of wedding planners. Ultimately, she had to put herself and her business first. Because no one else would.

"Look, Siegfried, you're a great guy, but I think we should keep our relationship strictly professional," Paige said, trying to disguise the longing in her voice. "I mean, since I'm technically your employee, it wouldn't be right."

"But you don't work for me," he said, sounding confused.

"Yes, but I am employed by your family, and Bebe made it clear I'm to run everything by you because you are paying the bills," Paige said. "I don't want to jeopardize what could be a big break for my business. I'm sure you understand."

Another guy might have agreed or written her off or maybe even have promised to call after the event she was hired to produce was over. But not Siegfried. When she dared to look at him, he just appeared puzzled, as if they weren't even speaking the same language.

She wanted nothing more than to wipe that expression off his face, preferably with her lips, but before she could be tempted any further, her phone buzzed. Glancing down at it, Paige was horrified to discover she'd spent an entire hour dancing with this guy.

"Sorry," she said, immediately changing into professional mode. "I have to run. I've got another appointment."

She turned to the door, wondering briefly how it had gotten closed because she didn't remember Siegfried shutting it behind him. Lifting the latch, she thrust it forward only to nearly run into Godfrey, who was right outside.

Paige eyed the butler askance. Was he listening at the door? Standing watch? But his white brows lifted as though daring her to accuse him of anything.

"Mrs. Maitland requested that I deliver this to you," he said, bowing his head just enough to make it appear that he was her servant when they both knew he was barely deigning to speak to her.

"What is it?" Paige asked, with one eye on the afternoon agenda she was scrolling through on her phone.

"It is an invitation to the Summers-Wainwright wedding."

"What?" Paige did a double take. "Really?" Talk about the wedding of the year. Those people were seriously rich, and Paige would love to get a look at their event.

"Really," Godfrey said, in that dry tone of his. "Mrs. Maitland has replied that Mr. Siegfried will be representing the family, with you as his plus one."

"What?" Paige asked, blinking at the butler.

"Shall I produce a megaphone or a hearing aid, or would you like me to text you this information?" Godfrey asked.

Biting her cheek, Paige shook her head.

"Very well," Godfrey said. "Mrs. Maitland suggested that Mr. Siegfried might need some experience before entering the realm of social engagements of this sort, and she would like you to guide him through a 'practice run,' as she worded it, dancing and all."

Paige felt a twinge of panic at that news. She'd barely been able to tear herself away from dancing with Good-looking Guy here in her office. She couldn't imagine waltzing with him, decked out in his tux, at some glamorous, romantic venue sprinkled with fairy dust far beyond even Zoe's imaginings.

How would she keep strictly to business?

But then Paige remembered that the boy genius would never emerge from his lab long enough to attend, leaving her to go solo and observe everything with the practiced eye of a professional, not the starry eye of a participant.

"Okay," she said, snatching up the invitation.

"Sounds like a plan," Siegfried said from the doorway.

Paige threw him a smile before she realized that it *did* sound like a plan, one hatched by Bebe and her butler. And maybe even her grandson.

But that was just crazy thinking. Right?

CHAPTER TWENTY-ONE

Was it a plan? Siegfried wasn't so sure, but he was getting desperate. When his grandmother had suggested the dancing lesson, he'd jumped at the chance even though normally he wouldn't be caught dead trying to move to music, especially in front of anyone else.

But if Bebe had been surprised at his quick agreement, she didn't comment. Siegfried eyed Godfrey curiously and wondered if his grandmother, like everyone else, had suddenly taken an interest in his love life. Or lack of it.

But Godfrey didn't blink. And Bebe hadn't brought up the subject, let alone attempted any encouragement and interference, so he figured she was too oblivious to everything around her to notice. Besides, she had long ago given up trying to force him to socialize.

And she seemed pretty involved in his sister's wedding. Although Hilde didn't complain about much, being the most laid-back of the Maitlands, that also made her susceptible to being pushed around. Not that Bebe pushed anyone around, but it was hard to say no to her.

And sometimes, Bebe didn't give her grandchildren a choice, like the "practice run" Siegfried just had been assigned without his input. In this case, however, he was more than willing to go along. Any opportunity to see Paige was a good thing, even if he had to do it at some society event.

He'd rather see her alone, and as he watched her go, he wracked his brain for some excuse to get together. But it seemed as though he always did better when his brain was not involved, like with her in his arms. In the moonlight.

He'd tried lunch. And dinner. Maybe another dance lesson? A discussion of the cost projection of Hilde's big event? Mia's job? With a grunt of satisfaction, Siegfried rushed past Godfrey to get to the garages before anyone else could commandeer the cars.

He was in luck. And on his way downtown, he kept up a steady conversation with Arthur, so he wouldn't be distracted from his goal. The man actually was pretty funny, with wry observations on everyone in the household whom Siegfried so often ignored.

A new sort of awareness clung to him as Siegfried took the public elevator to the company's upper floors, instead of his basement lab. He began to wonder if concentrating all his energies on his projects had been a mistake.

Maybe it had been the safest route when he was a kid, totally out of place among his college peers and facing either condescension or jealousy from his professors. But he was an adult now.

There was more to life than the climate-controlled environments where he spent most of his time. Like sunny afternoons and starry skies and Paige. Maybe Kevin was right, and he needed to quit working so much.

His father and grandfather had always made time for him, even if it was in the lab under the house, helping them with their inventions. But they always put him first. And maybe it was time for him to put something—someone—ahead of his own creations. Could he replace Project Paige with just Paige? It was a mind-altering concept.

Siegfried tried not to get lost in that thought as he walked through reception, greeting a surprised Latasha by name. Willow was just as surprised to see him when he strode into her office.

"You don't have a meeting today," she said.

"I know, but I wanted to talk to you. In person." Siegfried realized that he rarely spoke to his assistant, even though she obviously would have a female perspective on his current problems. As with the rest of the office staff, he hadn't really noticed her, but now he saw that she was pretty in a pre-Raphaelite way. And she'd certainly stayed longer than any other assistant he'd ever had.

"Okay," she said, looking wary as Siegfried dropped into the seat across from her. Had he ever sat here? Maybe he should take some time to have a conversation with her, like he had Arthur.

"I really appreciate you, Willow," he said. "Is Blake paying you enough?"

Her eyes widened behind the thick glasses she was wearing today. "Actually, I handle my own compensation and just have you sign off on it."

Siegfried loosed a stunned laugh. "Good," he said. Still, he vowed to check more closely all the papers she put in front of him, just in case Blake tried to slip something past him. Or her. But he suspected there wasn't much that got by Willow.

"By the way, your grandmother called and claimed you are committed to a wedding?" she said.

"Yes, go ahead and put it on my schedule."

"Seriously?"

"Seriously," Siegfried said.

She studied him from behind those glasses. "Are you feeling all right?"

Siegfried nodded. He *was* feeling all right. For once, he was eating and sleeping and living a life outside the lab. But he still had a lot of changes to make, starting right now. He leaned forward.

"I'm going to need a phone, a stripped-down one," he said. "The kind that is untraceable and paid up front."

Willow's eyes widened again. "Are you planning a crime?"

"Ha. No. I'm going to call someone." Hopefully.

"Ohhhkaay." Willow looked even more wary. Or was it agitated? He was never good at reading people.

"Oh, and one more thing," he said. "We need to find a job for Mia."

She blinked owlishly at him. "Blake won't like it."

Was that a warning or a protest? Either way, Siegfried didn't care. "I know," he said, grinning at the thought of his cousin's displeasure. He rarely got an opportunity to give Blake a little of his own.

Willow grinned right back at him, and for the first time outside of the lab, Siegfried felt like he was on a team, working toward a common goal that didn't involve code or any type of programming. Even if it was a bit malicious.

"What did you have in mind?" Willow asked.

Siegfried shrugged.

"Hmm." She turned to her computer screen and started scrolling through the company roster. "How about director of marketing?"

"Who's director of marketing?"

"One of Blake's slick cronies."

Siegfried frowned. "Does he do a good job?"

"Not good enough to justify his salary or his smarmy behavior."

"Great," Siegfried said. "Let's knock him down to second in command and make Mia his boss."

Willow looked at him, and they shared another conspiratorial smile. Then Siegfried leaned forward and gave his assistant a first-ever high five.

After rolling out of bed at an absurdly early hour, Mia hardly had time to change into her brand-new business clothes, short skirt, tight jacket, and Louboutins, all black, of course, before the car took her to meet with Siegfried's assistant, Willow.

The poor girl was one of those all-natural types with loose hair and clothes who fairly screamed for a makeover. But Mia kept quiet and listened. And when informed of her new position and its salary, she looked the girl straight in the eye. "I'm not going to be just a name with a title," she said.

Willow didn't blink. "Good. I'll get you an assistant who knows the business well." She paused. "But if I were you, I wouldn't ask for any help from the Assistant Director. Or your brother."

Mia snorted. "You got that right." She shared a look with the other woman, as if an understanding had been reached.

And Mia felt such a ridiculous rush of power and pleasure that she nearly pitched over when she stood up on her high heels.

But she managed to 'walk the walk' into her office and breeze through her introduction to Mr. Assistant Director, Sean Davis. Looking good and talking even better, Davis seemed to take her arrival in stride. But a lifetime of dealing with her brother made her suspicious of all that goodwill.

Sure enough, when Mia made it clear that she was here to work, not just collect a salary, his smile faltered. He recovered himself quickly, flashing his super-white teeth at her, but then excused himself to make a call in his own office.

And since Mia had learned during her difficult childhood it was best to know who's doing what, especially where she was concerned, she sat down at her big desk and hacked into his private call.

Although she'd missed the initial greeting, there was no mistaking the sound of her brother's voice. Or his outrage.

"That does it. I am so done with that fool. Now," Blake said.

Was he calling her a fool? Mia flushed with anger. But they had been done with each other long ago, so that didn't sound right.

"How soon can you get rid of her?" Davis asked.

"Don't worry about her," Blake said. "She won't last long. She won't be able to handle it, and even if she does, she'll be history, along with my cousin."

Mia's eyes narrowed at that claim, and she could almost see Blake's sneer as he paused before lowering his voice. "It's time to institute Operation Ouster."

Mia had to keep from snorting at these two acting like secret agents. Had they watched too many Bond movies or what?

"But it's earlier than you planned. Are you sure you have enough shares?" Davis asked.

"I've managed to buy more shares, but it's all about getting the votes. I just have to talk the rest of the family idiots into assigning their votes to me," Blake said.

When the call ended, Mia leaned back in her power chair.

She'd never been too fond of Siegfried, having spent most of her life envying the star of the family, with his loving parents and doting grandparents.

But he'd always been preferable to Blake, who could be counted on to screw everyone, either figuratively or literally. It was no surprise that her brother wanted to get rid of her. She knew too much about him and his ways for him to be comfortable with her around.

So what was he up to now? Whatever he was doing, Mia didn't have to consider her own allegiance. She was strictly with Siegfried, especially since she couldn't hold onto this job without him.

Blake had always underestimated her, but she wasn't about to underestimate him. They had grown up in the same toxic environment, and she'd learned a few tricks from him in the process.

Devious didn't even begin to describe him, so she figured he knew everything that went on here and used all that information to his advantage. He'd always preferred manipulation, blackmail, and spying to doing any real work.

So instead of picking up the phone, Mia picked up herself and made her way to Willow's office while typing a text into her cell. But she never pushed "send." Once she reached Willow's desk, she discreetly showed the message to Siegfried's assistant, without saying a word out loud:

What's Operation Ouster?

CHAPTER TWENTY-TWO

The wedding of the year was approaching way too fast. Although Paige usually remained calm in the face of calamities, she was starting to feel frazzled, while Zoe seemed unfazed. But, then, Zoe didn't have to deal with the Maitlands.

Although calls from the household had dwindled, Bebe had suggested more dance lessons for Siegfried, so he could rumba and fox trot with the best of them. Wary of getting up close and personal with Good-looking Guy again, Paige had sent a professional. The middle-aged one. Who was married.

Not that Paige cared, but she didn't want some ballroom bimbo to get her claws in the rich, handsome heir. After all, she had to look after her clients. And Bebe counted on her to keep things running smoothly.

At least that's what Paige told herself.

But things weren't running smoothly. The world's worst bride-to-be still didn't have anything to wear to the biggest event of her life. After several failed attempts to get her to a bridal shop, Paige had finally decided to bring the shop to her.

Having arranged with one of the premier stores to bring a selection of gowns out to the house, Paige worried that her client still wouldn't show. In fact, she approached her office in the mansion fully expecting to find it empty.

But, apparently, Paige's repeated reminders to both Hilde and her grandmother had done the trick. When the dresses arrived, so did the Maitlands, and the room was transformed into a fairyland of white tulle and satin and everything in between.

Although the salespeople were more than happy to oblige wealthy clients, Hilde wasn't very obliging. She stared placidly as each possibility was presented to her and enthused over. Then she started biting a fingernail.

And they think Siegfried is the socially awkward family member, Paige thought, trying not to frown at that injustice. But when Paige tried to move things along, Hilde did what she always did when faced with a decision.

She asked for Paige's preference.

Early on, Paige had claimed that it didn't matter what she liked, but what Hilde liked. If the bride wanted input, Paige happily would steer her toward choices that would most suit her.

Hilde had listened quietly, then pressed Paige for her favorite. Invariably, Hilde settled on what Paige chose. And Paige's initial guilt had given way to a simple relief that any decisions at all were being made.

Paige stifled a sigh. She'd selected the time, the decorations, the tuxes, the menu, the flowers, the table settings, the music, the cake, and seemingly everything else—far more than any other event she ever planned.

But what kind of bride didn't enjoy picking her own gown? Pasting on a smile, Paige selected a few she thought would be most flattering. At Bebe's instigation, they were tried on. And then dismissed.

Hilde didn't appear to be enjoying herself at all. Maybe she wanted something different, but was afraid to speak up? Paige rooted through the racks the shop had sent for something really offbeat. She pulled out a gauzy taupe number that looked more funerary than celebratory.

Everyone, including the salesgirls, eyed it dubiously.

Okay, no. "Would you like something in a different color? Red? Champagne?" Paige asked.

"Would you?" Hilde asked.

Uh, no. "I usually suggest going with the traditional, but it's your wedding, Hilde. You can wear whatever you want." Within reason. Paige couldn't imagine Bebe going along with a leotard or a Star Trek uniform. Or Mack painting something on his nude bride.

If he even existed. Or could paint.

"Would you feel more comfortable in something more artistic? Or from a historical period?" This wasn't a themed wedding, but Paige was getting desperate. She did not want to call another shop. And another. Or Vera Wang personally. As if she could.

Hilde chewed on her fingernail. "Which one do you like best?"

Paige drew in a deep breath and studied the myriad of designs before pulling out a silky, flowing number that fit her image of Hilde. "I think you would look incredible in this one."

She turned with a hopeful smile, but Hilde eyed her with brows furrowed. "No. Which one would you choose for yourself?"

"Me?" Paige had to swallow a snort as she tried to compose an appropriate response. After all, it wouldn't do for the wedding planner to admit she not only was never marrying but didn't believe in weddings. Somehow, she couldn't imagine that bit of information being good for her business.

But, as always, Paige found herself giving in to Hilde just to get things moving. Even the salespeople were looking desperate by this point. So Paige grabbed the nearest gown. "This one."

"Really?" Hilde asked in a skeptical tone.

"No, no." Bebe's voice was muffled by mounds of material, but she stepped out from behind the racks to hold up an off-white confection that made Paige's mouth drop open.

It was so *not* her. It was poufy. It was princessy. It was a ball gown, for God's sake. And yet, the sight of the simple, unadorned bodice meeting the billowing tulle made imaginary music swell. And scented breezes blow. And rose petals fall around her feet. She gaped at Bebe, who was smiling beatifically, and blinked in wonder.

Bibbidi bobbidi boo.

The business was growing so much that Paige and Zoe were forced to hire another full-time employee along with more part-timers to handle all the events they were getting. It was obvious to both of them that word of mouth about the upcoming wedding of the year was responsible.

But the increasing workload gave Paige little time to handle her unofficial duties as general go-to girl for the Maitland household, and oddly enough she found that she missed that craziness. She couldn't remember the last time she'd had a decent meal, let alone one in the boisterous, embracing atmosphere of the Maitland dining room, where anything was possible, including an appearance by Siegfried.

Okay, maybe she missed those chance encounters with good-looking, good guy. But it's not as though she'd heard from him since their dance lesson. Okay, maybe she had told him to back off in the nicest way possible, but still...

Even if she hadn't, Paige couldn't picture anyone ever prying him from the lab, and she was way too busy to do it. Yet she couldn't help wondering whether the guy was eating and sleeping. And if so, with whom.

So when she got a call from the mansion, Paige felt a rush of pleasure, like that of connecting with an old friend. Even the sound of Godfrey's accent was welcome, although he didn't seem inclined to chat. He simply reported that her presence was required at dinner.

Despite overwhelming evidence to the contrary, Paige nursed a hope that the boy genius wanted to see her. But when she tried to pump Godfrey for information, all she got was the advice to "dress casually."

"What?" she asked, baffled by that comment. It's not like she'd seen anyone in white tie and tails when she'd been eating there before.

"Perhaps flat shoes or trainers would be in order," Godfrey said.

"What?"

"I'm increasingly concerned about your hearing," the butler said before hanging up without further explanation.

Paige thought about ringing Bebe to ask her what was going on, but that was usually a futile gesture. Maybe she was expected to tour the new, improved gardens. If only she wasn't being summoned because of a *problem* with the new, improved gardens—or the landscapers.

Even that prospect failed to dampen her spirits, and Paige rearranged her schedule so she could drive out to the house. But when she arrived, she found her office empty. In fact, it looked kind of lonely, as though chastising her for staying away.

She was just about to head out in search of Godfrey or Bebe when Mia breezed in, dropping a huge designer bag as well as a briefcase on the floor.

"Hey, hang on a minute while I change, will you?" the heiress asked as she walked into the adjoining bath.

Had Mia taken over her office? Paige felt a twinge of disappointment even though she could make no real claim to it. She walked around the place, lovingly running a hand over the dust-free surfaces, gazing out at the amazing view, and trying to remember why she'd quit using the space.

Mia emerged, having exchanged her tight skirt for a pair of equally tight jeans and her five-inch heels for a pair of flats. Now Paige seriously wondered what was going on. Were they having a picnic?

"Come on," Mia said, grabbing her arm and pulling her from the room. Paige was too flustered to do anything except go along.

Had she really missed this Maitland craziness? Well, maybe, she thought, smiling in spite of herself as the heiress dragged her through the house and into the gardens.

They looked gorgeous. All the old, overgrown brush had been cleared away and new plantings put in their place. The stone wall and the flagstone paths had been repaired and others laid, winding through the foliage like secret passages.

Paige gawked, awestruck by the changes, though she let Mia continue to lead. But when they reached the newly restored gate, she dug in her heels. That's where the improvements— and the land itself—ended.

But Mia didn't seem to get that. "Come on," she said. "Let's go for a walk on the beach."

Paige eyed the heiress in horror. "Is this about the job? Because I swear Siegfried said—"

But Mia wouldn't let her finish, and the next thing she knew Paige was being dragged down the cliff, all her former fears about being murdered by the heiress returning.

Once again, she didn't have a phone to call for help. And even if she could find the secret lab, she didn't have a heeled shoe to bang on the door.

When she finally gave up struggling with Mia, Paige realized the trip wasn't so bad now that she was dressed more appropriately. In fact, Mia seemed to know the best route to take to the bottom, and they made their way without incident. No falls. No slides. No tumbling rocks.

Once there, Paige just faced the prospect of her companion drowning her or abandoning her in some underground cavern. Hadn't Mia claimed the cliffs were riddled with them?

"You don't have your cell, do you?" Mia asked.

Paige was tempted to lie, but the answer must have shown on her face because Mia appeared placated. For now.

"Good. I wanted to talk to you alone," she said.

Paige thought it more likely that the heiress wanted to *get her alone* since they could have spoken privately in the gardens or in the office or on the phone. She tensed.

"Without any possibility of being overheard by anyone—or anything," Mia added.

Paige blinked. She would have thought the heiress was drunk or high, but Mia seemed perfectly coherent. In fact, she looked great.

She'd put on some weight, so she wasn't quite as anorexic-looking. Her hair was styled in a simpler cut with more subtle highlights, and her makeup was toned down, too, though she still had her long nails.

The better to scratch you with, Paige thought.

Mia inclined her head. "Let's actually take a walk in case anyone's watching."

Who would be watching?

Paige began to wonder just how deep the family crazy

went. When did eccentric and interesting turn into seriously mental? Had Mia gone off some meds?

But short of shrieking and heading back up the cliff, Paige had no alternative except to humor her companion. So she fell into step with the heiress. At least for awhile.

"By the way, I owe you a thanks," Mia said, which made Paige stop dead and gape at her.

A nudge from the heiress got her going again.

"You're the first person in my life who saw promise in me beyond a party girl, sex partner, high-profile name, or charge account," Mia said. "And you not only saw that, but you acted like it was normal. And you acted like Siegfried would think it was normal, too."

Paige put one foot in front of the other while trying to hide her astonishment.

"He and Willow gave me the job, and I've been really working hard, but loving it. You know what I mean?"

Paige nodded, some of the strain easing out of her body.

"But I've also got to deal with Blake's crap, which is why I wanted to take this walk away from everything. He's got the entire office's communications wired. I'm sure of it. And probably the house, too."

Paige tensed again. Okay, maybe the guy was a jerk, but spying? On everyone? "Really?"

Mia eyed her askance. "Believe me, I've been a lifelong victim of Blake's maneuvering, and even I was shocked by what he's planning."

So Blake was planning something to do with the company. Why should that concern Paige? It took her only a moment to come up with the answer. "He's going to fire me?" she asked, blurting out the fear she had nearly forgotten.

Mia snorted. "Worse. He's going to fire Siegfried."

CHAPTER TWENTY-THREE

Okay, so maybe Blake wasn't going to fire Siegfried, just turn the boy genius into even more of a powerless slave to the family's interests, sort of like the robots he was designing. But that was bad enough.

Drawing on her college courses, Paige shared with Mia what she knew about the structures of companies in general, though she was no expert on the one owned by the Maitlands. But even to her skeptical ears, it sounded like Mia and Siegfried's assistant had uncovered an internal takeover plot.

And from what she'd heard about Blake, it wasn't hard to imagine him forcing his cousin out as CEO and putting himself in the guy's place. Horrified, Paige wanted to go find Siegfried immediately to tell him what was up. But it was plain which cousin had the better head for business, and no one wanted Blake to realize they were on to him. Hence, the secrecy.

Because even if they foiled Blake's plans this time, there would always be a next time—unless they managed to turn the tables on him completely. Willow had floated some ideas for Mia to run by Paige since the three of them could hardly meet without drawing notice.

It looked like they were the only people who had Siegfried's back—and the wherewithal to act upon their suspicions. So, with Paige's input, a scheme was hatched, though most of the responsibility for its success rested on Mia.

A month ago or even an hour ago, Paige would never have put Siegfried's fate into the heiress's hands. But now... Well, she still didn't want to, but what else could she do? Mia seemed far better suited to the cutthroat world of the company than the man behind its breakthroughs, even if they could coax him away from the computer long enough to take control of the situation.

Keeping up the appearance of a casual outing, the two

climbed back up the side of the cliff, which wasn't easy. But Paige figured if Mia could do it, she could. She sure wasn't about to go knocking on the door of the hidden lab.

In fact, Paige had to banish all hope of running into Siegfried. She didn't want to be put in the position of hiding information from him, especially information about Blake. And Mia. And Willow. And his own future.

She didn't even want to stay for dinner, but there was no way to avoid the gathering once she was spotted. At least Mia took off, so Paige didn't have to worry about the possible return of the heiress' sharp tongue.

With Mia out of the picture, Paige was able to relax. Everyone in the dining room greeted her like a long-lost relative, and soon she was catching up with Uncle Otto and Lorenzo and Linde and all the hangers-on.

Without an extended family of her own, Paige enjoyed being welcomed into this one. Even if they were a motley group of eccentrics, they made her feel wanted in a way she never had before.

Like the house itself, they provided something that seemed an awful lot like the home she'd never known. But in the midst of their warm embrace, she couldn't help but worry about the one guy who wasn't there.

Paige jerked awake at the sound of a voice in her ear. Scrambling to awareness, she lifted her head and yanked at the headset attached to it. Had she fallen asleep at the keyboard like Siegfried?

The crick in her neck, the sun peeking through the blinds, and the sight of the t-shirt she was wearing gave her the answer. She groaned.

"Paige?"

Snatching the headset up again, Paige put it back in place while trying to force her aching body into a sitting position.

"Are you there?" Zoe asked, her tone tinged with concern.

"Sure," Paige muttered. She cleared her throat. "Of course."

"Okay," Zoe said, sounding unconvinced.

"Is there something wrong?"

"I don't know. Is there?" Zoe asked. "I'm just calling for the morning schedule update, even though it's Sunday, and any sane woman would be in bed."

"Right," Paige said, getting her cursor going, so she could see the day's to-do list.

"Right?" Zoe's voice rose. "Are you finally facing the truth that we are taking on too many clients?"

Paige groaned again. Lately, Zoe had been complaining about the hours and wanting to refuse some of the smaller jobs. But Paige had worked so hard to build her business that she hated to turn away any.

Yet even her organizational skills could not create more time, and she had begun to feel the strain, too. Glancing at today's timetable, she saw the Summers-Wainwright reception listed, and her heart started pounding.

"Are you handling the Summers-Wainwright?" Paige fairly shrieked, even as she swung round to look for her tablet, her phone, or notes of any kind on an event she didn't remember. But her movement dislodged a pile of materials that fell onto more piles of materials.

"Uh, no. I don't think we've gone that upscale yet," Zoe said. "Are you all right? You aren't having a stroke or something, are you?"

Paige let her head fall forward onto the tiny desk in the tiny work area of her tiny apartment. "I'm okay," she said, eyeing the efficiency that was anything but. When had the place started looking like something out of Hoarders-R-Us?

Oh yeah. When she quit using the office Bebe had provided, while taking on all the clients Bebe's reputation had provided. As if that weren't depressing enough, the thought of that luxurious space spurred a longing for the mansion and everyone in it, including the good-looking, good guy she was trying to avoid.

Paige was tempted to call and have Arthur drive over to cart all her stuff out to that elegant room with the attached suite and move in, as Zoe had advised. But what would be the point? The wedding was only a week away, and once the big night ended, so did her tenuous connection to the Maitlands.

Paige closed her eyes against that reality. Despite her hectic schedule and the excitement over her success, she'd had a nagging sensation that something was missing. Although she'd refused to acknowledge it, now she felt absurdly homesick for a home that wasn't hers and the guy she was avoiding, for her good or his. She couldn't remember which.

"Well, I don't blame you for being confused," Zoe said. "We've got way too much on our plate, Paige. And when the Maitland do is over, we need to sit down and reassess."

She sounded serious. Was she bailing? Paige lifted her head.

"But in the meantime, you have an event scheduled where you are required to do nothing except have a good time," Zoe said.

"I don't know," Paige replied automatically as she remembered the invitation Bebe had foisted on her—and its purpose. A "practice run," the older woman had called it, and at the time Paige had been wary. Now she was even more wary. She hadn't heard anything from Mia lately, but neither had she gotten any reports about changes at the company.

While the prospect of spending an evening with Siegfried had an immediate effect upon Paige's heart—and other long-neglected parts of her body—she didn't like the idea of concealing anything from him, especially up close and personal and dancing in the dark.

"What's not to know?" Zoe asked. "Hey, I can understand not wanting to go to another reception, but this one comes with the promise of great food, wine, and entertainment—all supplied by someone else. Or is this about the handsome, rich guy any sane woman would love to accompany?"

"It's complicated," Paige muttered.

"Right," Zoe said, scoffing. "Look, Paige, I'm worried about you. You're getting as bad as he is, taking no time off, obsessing about work..."

Paige opened her mouth only to shut it again when she realized Zoe had a point, although not the intended one. She wouldn't have to worry about revealing any secrets to Siegfried unless she actually were with the guy. And his track record for showing up wasn't good. What made her think he was going to leave his robots for her, even briefly?

"Okay, I'll go," she said, cutting off Zoe's lecture. And if she felt a tingly sense of anticipation, it was solely due to an evening of freedom, not the possible appearance of an extremely unlikely companion.

"Good," Zoe said. "I expect you to take off the entire day. You aren't even allowed to schmooze the vendors there."

Paige wasn't so sure about that, especially since she probably would be on her own, but she kept that fact to herself. After promising a full report later, she said goodbye and began cleaning up both the apartment and herself.

Although her job necessitated a certain appearance, Paige took the opportunity to get an overdue mani-pedi and bought a pricey new dress. And by the time the evening approached, she was more than ready for a night out.

Sticking the invitation in her clutch and leaving her headset behind, she turned toward the door just as she heard someone outside. She put an eye to the peephole and fell back to slump against the wall in surprise.

Okay, so maybe she'd been hoping that Bebe would send Arthur to ferry her to the reception since she was representing the family. But she certainly hadn't expected to see Siegfried Maitland at her door. Should she feign ignorance? Illness? Claim she had to work? Or just fail to answer?

"Paige?"

It was him all right. Paige would know that warm, wonderful voice anywhere. It lured her in, making her forget all of her reservations. Against all odds, he was here, and Paige couldn't suppress a surge of delight.

She opened the door, and there he was, sporting not only the best-fitting tuxedo ever but also a haircut, a clean shave, and the handsomest face she'd ever seen. She felt like throwing herself into his arms and never leaving.

She settled on smiling and locking up.

"Where's Arthur?" she asked.

"Oh, he's got the night off."

What? Had Siegfried hired a car? The probability of that piece of planning made her wonder whether they were taking the bus in their evening clothes. Or sharing a skateboard. She eyed him skeptically.

"I do have my license, you know," he said, with a grin that did something to her insides. Was this the new, improved Siegfried, or had he been replaced by a robot double?

So maybe the trip was a little harrowing because the boy wonder wasn't used to driving, license or no. But when they arrived at their destination and he took her arm to lead her into one of San Francisco's most famous landmarks, Paige decided she didn't care if he was an alien clone, as long as he stayed by her side.

Sure, her job took her to amazing locations, but some places still had the power to awe. And she hadn't been to this elegant historic building even in a work-related capacity because it was way too pricey for any of her clients.

Yet, here she was, like Cinderella going to the ball, or at least to the ballroom. And it was all she could do not to gawk. From the filigreed elevator doors to the marbled foyer to the gilded ceiling, every detail was breathtaking. And Paige wasn't one to lose her breath—except maybe around the guy beside her.

She couldn't really tell whether it was Siegfried or the atmosphere, but when she saw the massive fireplace and towering windows, sparkling chandeliers and centerpieces, elegant linens and table settings, Paige knew what Zoe would say.

Bibbidi bobbidi boo.

CHAPTER TWENTY-FOUR

When she finally came up for air, Paige noticed the envious stares of other women and heard the curious whispers about her escort. And she was only too happy to prove wrong those who called the guy socially awkward as they moved among the ranks of the city's elite.

Maybe Siegfried wasn't as smooth as Blake or most of the other males in his tax bracket, but to Paige, that could only be a good thing. And when he turned his laser-like attention on her, all she could do was bask in its glow.

Luckily, their table was nearly empty, a fact that might disappoint an event planner, but suited Cinderella just fine. Left to themselves, they sat close in the glow of the flickering lights and Siegfried eyed her seriously.

"I have something to tell you."

Had he missed her? Was he going to ask her for a date after the wedding? A girl could hope, couldn't she? Paige leaned in, nodding for him to continue.

"I have a phone number," he said.

Paige couldn't help laughing at her ridiculous expectations. This was Siegfried, she reminded herself, and all bets were off.

"Okay," she said, pulling out her phone to put in the digits before turning it off.

"But don't give it to anyone else," he said. "It's just for... you."

The way he spoke, in a low voice intended solely for her ears, had Paige's emotions doing another one eighty. This was Siegfried, she reminded herself again. And if he never behaved like other guys, that wasn't always a bad thing.

They dined on delicate appetizers and gourmet entrees, exchanging bites of rack of lamb and glazed ahi tuna, bent their heads together, talked, and laughed. And not once did the boy genius try to write code—or anything else—on the napkins.

In fact, when he did lift his hand, he placed it over Paige's and entwined their fingers, a simple act that robbed her of any vestige of good sense.

"I'm a hands-on kind of guy," he whispered, making her pulse leap as he rubbed his thumb against her skin. Maybe it was time she had another demonstration of his manual dexterity...

They toasted the bride and groom with the most expensive champagne Paige had ever tasted, and she actually ate her piece of the wedding cake, so exotic and rich that she felt like licking the crumbs off her plate. Or Siegfried's lips.

When they danced, they moved together seamlessly, as if no time had passed since the lesson. And Paige wondered whether absence really did make the heart grow fonder. Although leery of any saying involving that organ, she had the eerie sensation that they'd never been apart.

Paige shook her head. She'd always rolled her eyes at the couples who carried on about destiny and fate, but here and now, it didn't seem quite so crazy. She was floating on champagne and music and glittering lights in the most amazing venue with a guy who just got better and better.

Paige didn't even seek introductions to the kind of potential clients who could make her business—because business never crossed her mind. For once, she was living in the moment, all else forgotten except the magic of the night and the company.

She might be Cinderella, but it was Siegfried who'd been transformed. Although always rich and handsome, the boy genius had turned into an Armani-clad prince ready to waltz her across the floor instead of knock her down with his skateboard.

"So what happened?" Paige asked.

He lifted his dark brows in question.

"Your prompt appearance. This. You," Paige said, swinging her arm to take in his hair, his clothes, and his undivided attention.

He smiled. "I realized that life's about balance, and nothing comes from working too hard."

The memory of waking up on her own keyboard that morning made Paige glance away. Maybe they both worked too hard.

"Work is important, especially when you love what you do," Siegfried said, as if reading her thoughts. "But I discovered other things are important, too."

The hushed tone of his voice made her look at him again.

"Like spending time with people you love."

Paige blinked. Whoa. Slow down there. Was he saying what she thought he was saying? That was crazy, right? Too much, too soon from a guy who had more experience with robots than people.

But something in his eyes made Paige swallow her quips and protests. In fact, she had a hard time breathing at the thought of the possibilities she saw there. But she retained enough sense to know that possibilities were not probabilities.

When Siegfried was present, he was oh, so present. Yet how often did that happen? Paige knew how unreliable he was. Sure, he was not the kind of unreliable that her father had been, but enough to make her think twice.

She had spent way too much time guarding her heart to just hand it over, even to this good-looking, good guy. Best guy, Paige amended. He might not be the best man at his sister's wedding, but he was the best guy she'd ever known.

Maybe he hypnotized her with that guileless gaze. But Paige found herself going along as he took her home, slipped her into the Maitland mansion without being seen, and slipped her out of her clothes in that great big bed of his, where best-looking, best guy proved he was the best at... everything.

Paige snuggled deeper under the covers, amazed at how comfortable and roomy her cheap mattress felt after a good night's sleep. She dozed happily until she realized that no amount of rest could conjure her sense of well-being.

Her eyes flew open, and one look at the intricately carved

molding above her head proved that she wasn't in Kansas anymore. Or Indiana. Or her own tiny apartment in San Francisco.

There was no mistaking the big, soft bed and the even bigger room, far more luxuriously appointed than anywhere she'd ever lived. And then memory flooded back.

Sighing with pleasure, Paige turned, expecting to see the broad back or the handsome face of Siegfried Maitland, a genius in every sense of the word. Perhaps another demonstration of how good he was with his hands was in order, she thought dreamily.

But he was gone.

Rolling over, Paige saw only rumpled blankets. She called out his name, wondering whether he was in the shower. Although he didn't answer, the prospect of Tall, Dark, and Wet made her wrap herself in a sheet and go looking.

But there was no sign of him in the bath or any of the attached rooms that appeared completely unlived in. Nor had he left a note of any kind, even one with thanks and cab fare. Paige frowned.

Okay, so this was Siegfried. Did she think that one night would make him a new man? Well, yes. She'd been hoping. But when she saw his tux jacket thrown across a chair, abandoned, there was no denying reality.

Her prince had turned back into a pumpkin.

Glancing at her own hopelessly crumpled dress, Paige cringed at the Walk of Shame she would have to make this morning. But nothing of Siegfried's would fit her, and she'd never had the foresight to put some extra clothes in her so-called office.

Resigned, she picked up the garment only to gape in horror at the space beneath. With one hand holding the sheet to her naked body, she frantically dropped to the floor and began groping on her hands and knees, searching everywhere, including under the bed—for what wasn't there.

She sat back on her heels as the truth sank in: Her clutch was gone, and inside it was her phone.

Paige's lingering afterglow was replaced by panic at the thought of not having today's schedule. What time was it? Grabbing her dress, she ran into the bathroom, pausing only long enough to splash some water on her face and run fingers through her hair.

She figured Siegfried was in the lab, so she'd just have to make her way down there while avoiding the other residents with their inevitable questions and gleeful insinuations. If only she didn't run into Godfrey, she thought with a groan. She was way too frazzled to deal with the butler's disdain.

Luckily, the mansion seemed strangely deserted, though it was early enough that people might be in bed or having breakfast. Skirting the main rooms, she headed straight for the elevator and slipped inside.

Only then did she wonder just how to behave when she found Siegfried. She didn't have a whole lot of experience with morning-afters, and she definitely had never experienced anything like the night before. But it wasn't like the guy was going to blow her off, right? Or forget her...

Just as she imagined that grim possibility, the doors opened, but Siegfried was nowhere to be seen. In fact, everything looked so different that for a moment she wondered whether she was in the right place.

Instead of the stark bright whiteness, she was met with a dim, pale light that made the place eerie. Or even eerier than usual.

The robots lay in various stages of assembly, but the parts and limbs were now in shadow like the detritus of some fastidious serial killer. Or New Age Frankenstein. And the silence of the deep underground space was unbroken except for the low hum of various machines.

It was way too creepy.

"Siegfried?" The word came out fainter than Paige intended, a mere squeak that did not travel well in the vast area. But before she could repeat herself more loudly, she heard something.

Stiffening, Paige squinted at the partitions and glassed-in areas and metal tables looming around her. Was there a slasher movie set somewhere like this? Because Paige felt a big old scream building.

And then the elevator doors started to close behind her.

Stifling the bottled-up shriek, Paige stepped back just in time. The doors stopped halfway open. But her sigh of relief was cut off by a sound of someone—or something—approaching.

Maybe the robots were taking over? Paige had no clue what Siegfried had programmed them to do. She peeked outside and relaxed at the sight of Tad, only to tense again when she saw his menacing expression.

"What are you doing here?" he asked. He looked her bedraggled dress up and down in a way that raised the hairs on her neck.

The guy always took his job too seriously, but Siegfried had reined him in. And facing him alone, Paige felt a new uneasiness. She was acutely aware of the fact that she had no purse, no phone, and not even a very dangerous heel on her shoe.

"I was looking for Siegfried."

"Don't come down here again."

At another time, Paige might have argued about his authority, but now she just pressed the elevator button. Nothing happened. Was the thing wonky, or did Tad have some kind of remote control over it?

"You think I don't know what goes on here?" he asked. "I've got eyes and ears everywhere. And perfect aim." He put a hand to rest on the gun at his side, and Paige's heart thudded.

"Are you threatening me?" She managed to force out the words in a strangled croak.

"I'm warning you," he said before the doors finally shut.

Slumping against the wall, Paige had a hard time breathing. Suddenly, the small space seemed even smaller, and she had the crazy fear that she'd been left in it to die. Or maybe she was going down to some lower level where Tad kept his torture devices.

When the elevator began moving upward, Paige nearly sobbed with relief, and she stumbled out, not caring who saw her. She made her shaky way to her office, but instead of providing sanctuary, the luxurious room seemed forbidding, and she wondered if there were hidden cameras or microphones everywhere.

Wasn't that why Mia wanted to walk on the beach? Paige shivered. But it was one thing to suspect Blake of monitoring phone calls from the house. It was quite another to imagine Tad watching video from every corner of the house, even the private areas. Like Siegfried's bedroom?

Paige didn't care to find out. She grabbed the landline and called a cab to meet her at the bottom of the drive. Then she made a quick exit, swinging by the garages to see if she'd left her clutch in the car.

But both Arthur and the vehicle were gone, probably in the service of another member of the household—or Siegfried himself. Paige wasn't willing to go there. Not now. Maybe not ever.

For all she knew her purse was in Tad's possession. She'd have to get a new phone, retrieve all her backed-up info from the cloud, and call Zoe to find out what she'd already missed.

The thought of Zoe waiting eagerly for a report of her evening off was nearly as bad as the thought of Siegfried. Sure, Cinderella had to walk back from the ball, bare-foot and hauling a pumpkin, but this whole experience just reaffirmed Paige's deep-seated belief.

Fairy tales were for fools.

CHAPTER TWENTY-FIVE

Siegfried didn't know what to expect as he walked into company headquarters. Not long ago he'd been lying in bed watching Paige sleep, marveling at his good fortune, and thinking about the most awesome night of his life.

In fact, he was looking forward to the most awesome morning of his life. Or at least he hoped they could pick up where they'd left off when they'd both finally succumbed to exhaustion—not the kind that came from staying up too long or doing too much work, but the kind that, well, Siegfried couldn't ever recall succumbing to before.

But then his phone had buzzed, the one no one knew about except Willow and Paige. He'd grabbed it in order not to wake her and was surprised to see a text from his assistant. Normally, he would have ignored it, especially considering where he was and what he was up to—or nearly up to.

But Willow didn't send him texts, and this one instructed him to come directly to the office without notifying anyone. Siegfried didn't know what kind of emergency would require his presence, but he was thinking maybe a lab break-in, or worse, an explosion, though he didn't deal with volatile chemicals like his father or grandfather had.

He did not expect a board meeting.

When Siegfried walked in, he would have turned around and walked out, except that his grandmother was there. And Mia. And Willow. Obviously, this was not your typical board meeting, and it didn't take him long to figure out what the emergency was.

Blake was trying to take over the company. And he was putting it to a vote. He'd even prepared handouts detailing the reasons to remove Siegfried as CEO.

Apparently, the branch of the Maitland family that had produced the inventions and made the money that the other members freely spent were no longer to have any say over their creations. And Blake was so sure of himself that he barely looked up when Siegfried entered.

"Oh, Siegfried, I'm afraid we weren't expecting you since you so rarely attend board meetings—or attend to business of any sort," he said. He flashed his white teeth in a smile intending to convey—what? Sympathy? Ruefulness? More likely, ruthlessness.

Blake turned to address the board members. "I think you've all received reports of the CEO's behavior. In addition to the breaches of security, missing data, and questionable connections, there is the usual failure to review documents necessary to the running of the company, missed meetings, etc."

"I was in the lab working," Siegfried said in a low tone.

Blake showed his expensively capped teeth again. "Whatever the reasoning behind these lapses, I'm afraid there are too many responsibilities that aren't being properly executed, which necessitates a change in leadership."

As if Blake's plans would benefit everyone, he smiled again. "And I'm sure we all agree that will leave you more time to devote to your area of expertise."

Siegfried couldn't believe the bastard was presenting himself as a reasonable alternative when his work record and motivations were suspect. Bebe always claimed Blake could sell ice in the Arctic, which made him a good representative for the face of the business. But had he fooled the board? And his own family?

Siegfried glanced around the table at the men and women who refused to look up from the files in front of them, let alone glance his way, and for a moment he wondered why he even cared. Hadn't he just been telling Paige that he worked too much? And without this burden, he could focus on the enjoyable part.

No meetings. No paperwork. No office.

Then he glanced at Blake and realized he couldn't give control of his father's and grandfather's legacy to someone who didn't value creating or work of any kind and who would sell his birthright for a few bucks.

With grim certainty, Siegfried made his decision, but who was with him? He didn't own enough shares to prevail without help.

Unfortunately, the only thing Blake excelled at was deceit and manipulation, so he probably had the majority. Who knows what he promised for votes from those who, one by one, pledged Blake their support while Siegfried watched helplessly.

The presence of Bebe, who usually avoided these things, didn't bode well. She wasn't as flighty as most people thought, but she'd never really concerned herself with the business. And her disapproval of Blake's lifestyle didn't mean he couldn't convince her to vote for the good of the company or some such nonsense. For all Siegfried knew, she'd signed her shares over to the president months ago.

He tried to catch Bebe's eye, but she seemed oblivious to his turmoil, and Siegfried braced himself as she finally spoke. When she voted down the proposal, he loosed a low whistle of stunned approval. But he wasn't the only one surprised by her actions.

Obviously, Blake was expecting a different response, for his confident smile vanished. "But, Grandmother," he began.

Bebe shook her head. Either she'd come to her senses or something had changed her mind, depriving Blake of a huge block of votes. Siegfried thought he saw a bead of sweat appear on his cousin's smooth forehead.

Blake turned to his sister, who had only a few shares. "Mia?" he asked. Was his tone indulgent, condescending, or desperate? Maybe a bit of all three, Siegfried decided.

"I vote no," she said. "Oh, and I'm voting all of Mom's shares, too."

"Mom?" Blake said, his carefully constructed facade cracking. "Your mother? *Our* mother?"

"Yes," Mia said in a businesslike manner that surprised Siegfried.

And Blake. He glanced around the room like a cornered animal. "That simply can't be. There must be some mistake."

"There's no mistake," Mia said.

Somehow the spoiled wild child had been transformed into a savvy professional. Mia's clothes might be a little edgy for the office, but otherwise, she was indistinguishable from other corporate types—until she spoke again.

"Epic fail, bro," she said, flashing her own expensive caps.

Blake looked like he was going to lunge over the table at her, but Bebe rose to her feet, putting a stop to Blake's sputtering and commanding everyone else's attention.

"Since the proposal has been voted down, I move that we accept the president's resignation."

"What the hell?" Blake screamed the obscenity, but Bebe ignored him.

"And in his place, I suggest we appoint my granddaughter Wellgunde, who will receive her MBA next month. She's more than willing to work with a CEO who focuses on laboratory results, not meetings."

Everyone seemed relieved to be able to kick Blake to the curb, even those he'd maneuvered into voting with him, whether by bribery or blackmail. But Blake wasn't going down quietly. He began shouting threats at everyone in the room, even his grandmother.

Siegfried rose to his feet, ready to have the ex-president escorted from the building, but that only drew his cousin's attention. Blake's face was practically crimson as he turned on Siegfried like a rabid dog.

"This is all her fault! Everything was on track until she started sticking her nose into my business. I should have taken Tad's advice and charged her with corporate espionage."

Siegfried froze. "What are you talking about?"

"I'm talking about that bitch you're screwing," Blake screamed, pointing a finger at Siegfried's chest. "I'm talking about the damn wedding planner!"

For once in his life, Siegfried didn't stop to think. He closed his fingers into a fist and swung at his cousin as hard as he could. There was a collective gasp from the board members as Siegfried astonished everyone, including himself.

But especially Blake.

The force of the blow against his jaw sent Blake sprawling back onto the table, scattering his detailed reports and sending chairs flying as people leapt out of the way.

Siegfried was vaguely aware of Willow calling for security, of his grandmother demanding that Blake behave, and of Mia admiring his handiwork. But mostly, he was aware of the throbbing pain in his bleeding knuckles.

"I'm not feeling well," Paige said into her headset.

"What? You're never sick!" Zoe shrieked. "What's wrong with you? Unless you are projectile vomiting, you are not leaving me in charge of the Maitland wedding."

What was wrong with her? Paige wasn't sure. All she knew was that she felt nauseated at the thought of stepping back into the fairy tale, of seeing everything that had upset her ordered life, the beautiful home, the welcoming people, the crazy family, and the guy who...

"You are so not sick."

Maybe it wasn't a verifiable disease, but Paige was heartsick, and she didn't like the feeling. She was used to being in control, and there was no controlling the Maitlands or anyone associated with them. The only way to avoid that emotional roller coaster was to get off.

"You're just scared," Zoe said. "You have to face him sooner or later."

"Uh, no," Paige said. She couldn't deal with it. She could handle missing flowers, drunken party guests, drugged-up DJs, and exploding cakes. But she could not handle the boy genius.

If she saw him again, especially dressed in his tux, Paige knew she'd be sucked back into the fantasy. She'd fallen for the romance, the candlelight, the music, the dancing—all the things she knew were contrived because she made a living contriving them.

And once she'd fallen, she'd found herself wanting the icing-covered, fairy-dust-sprinkled, glittering happily-ever-after that never was. She wasn't about to go there again.

"Maybe your big night didn't turn out as well as I hoped, but no date is perfect," Zoe said.

Paige snorted. "Okay, let's recap," she said. "He left me without a goodbye, without a note, without my purse, and with a psychotic peeping tom—who threatened me with a gun."

"He had an excuse," Zoe protested.

How can you possibly excuse all that? Sure, Mia had called and told her about the board meeting, and Paige was glad that Blake's plans had been foiled. But that didn't mean she wanted to get right back on the roller coaster.

Paige was afraid, all right. She was afraid to invest more time and energy and emotion into someone who couldn't return it, not because he was a bad guy. But because he was Siegfried.

"All guys are a pain. It's the nature of the beast," Zoe said.

Paige choked out a laugh. "Yeah, most guys go out drinking or don't remember a birthday. This one never leaves the lab and is liable not to remember... me."

The reality was that her best guy had forgotten her. Maybe it wasn't like her dad forgetting her, but Paige just couldn't sign up for a future of being forgotten.

"Oh, Paige," Zoe whispered. "I'm sorry."

Was Zoe sorry there was no animated movie ending? Or sorry to see her own illusions shattered?

"It's okay," Paige said, glad that her friend couldn't see her swollen eyes or tear-stained face.

It would be okay. Once today was over, Paige would put the whole experience behind her. She had her priorities straight again, having learned her lesson. Work would always be there, while Siegfried Maitland would not.

So Paige immersed herself in the details of upcoming events, rather than the wedding of the year. And when her phone buzzed, she hoped it wasn't Zoe with some Maitland emergency.

"Hello?"

"Where are you?" Bebe asked without preamble. Paige stifled a groan. She hadn't expected the older woman to notice her absence quite so soon, but she'd prepared a little speech about how everything would go smoothly with Zoe's oversight.

She'd barely opened her mouth when the elegant society matron raised her voice imperiously. "I've sent Arthur to fetch you," she said. "We have a problem."

Paige took a deep breath, but Bebe cut her off again.

"We can't find the bride."

By the time Paige got dressed and slathered makeup on her ravaged face, Arthur was waiting. And by the time she reached the mansion, time was running out. The guests would be arriving soon.

Even if the future success of her business wasn't riding on this one, Paige would have been frantic. As it was, she took control the minute she set foot out of the car. Bebe met her in the garages, and Paige insisted that they go directly to Hilde's hideaway.

"But no one answers, and the door is locked, dear," Bebe said. "We can hardly barge in."

"I'll barge in," Paige said, through gritted teeth. To placate Bebe, she added, "Just to make sure Hilde isn't ill or injured." Or that Mack hadn't murdered her and run off with her money.

But since Bebe had no real assistant or housekeeper, she didn't know where to find a set of keys to the apartments.

"Maybe Tad can shoot off the lock," Paige said dryly.

"Oh no," Bebe said. "Siegfried dismissed that dreadful man. And he had a company come sweep for bugs and cameras and that sort of thing."

Paige ignored the flutter in her chest at that good news and concentrated on the problem at hand. So, no guns. Maybe a crowbar? She glanced at Arthur, figuring he would be the best candidate for muscle, but then realized there was someone who really ought to have keys.

"What about the butler?" she asked.

"Yes! Go fetch Godfrey," Bebe said to Arthur.

"So you think he has a set?" Paige asked, relieved.

"Oh no," Bebe said. "But he can pick the lock."

Paige didn't know what to do with the knowledge that the Brit had access to any room in the house. *At least you aren't living here*, she told herself. And if she did, she'd get a deadbolt.

When the seemingly proper Englishman arrived, Paige wondered what they would do if Hilde and Mack had thought to install one, too. But Godfrey did not seem concerned.

"Good to see you are in charge again, miss," he said.

"I've always been in charge of the wedding," Paige said. So what if she'd bailed on the event itself?

Godfrey lifted his bushy brows. "Of the household."

Paige opened her mouth but decided there was no point in arguing. After today, she wouldn't see any of these people again. No more slacker butlers. No more fairy godmothers. No more crazy Maitlands and their crazy guests.

So why didn't that make her feel better?

Kneeling before the lock with an impressive array of tools, Godfrey soon had the thing sprung. Paige didn't even ask him where he'd acquired those skills.

The door swung inward, and a hush fell on those gathered outside, just as though they were breaking and entering. Or coming across a crime scene. Or both.

Finally, Paige stepped forward. "Hilde? Mack?" she called out, hoping that she wouldn't see anything too weird, alive or dead. But when she walked inside, she could only gape in astonishment at what was there.

The roof at the rear of the building was filled with skylights, so the golden glow of sunset bathed the room, a vast open space that smelled of paint and all its accessories. Had Paige suspected Mack of scamming them all without leaving behind a crayon doodle?

Well, she was wrong. Huge canvases were stacked against the walls, each one more interesting than the last. Swirls of colors and shapes and images of Hilde, glorious and glorified, filled most of them. Paige knew nothing about art, but she was awestruck.

"Lovely, aren't they?" Bebe asked, and Paige realized she was staring. She turned around to look for any sign of the couple.

"I believe this is what you are seeking," Godfrey said, plucking a note from the corner of an empty frame and handing it to Bebe.

"Dear Grandmother," she read aloud. "I know you wanted a big wedding, and I really tried to go along with it. But Mack feels it would be selling out to societal and commercial interests and a betrayal of his art and all that it represents."

Paige blinked, too stunned to draw a breath. Was she hearing what she thought she was hearing? All her hopes for her business, her precious showcase, the wedding of the year, were going down in flames? She swayed on her feet, a low sound of dismay escaping her tight throat, but Bebe kept reading.

"We're going to head down to an artist community in Mexico, where Mack can paint in a warmer environment, among the similarly gifted. I know you'll put the wedding plans to good use."

What? Paige choked back a cry of outrage. How? Was she supposed to substitute other clients for Hilde and Mack? In a celebration to be held at their own house? With their invited guests? It didn't work that way, except in Wackyland.

Bebe smiled brightly, seemingly unaffected by the news. "Well, she's right, of course. I'm sure something can be arranged." She turned to Godfrey. "You know what to do."

Paige sank onto a futon and buried her head in her hands. She didn't even have the strength to call Zoe. And the vendors. And the guests.

Clients cancelled. It happened, although rarely. And Paige pocketed her fee without a loss. But she'd put her heart and soul into something designed to impress the attendees and convince them to use her services.

Now, no one would be impressed. In fact, her name would be associated with a big, fat failure. She whimpered.

"Now, now, dear," Bebe said. "All will be well, you'll see. Let me get you a glass of water."

Paige heard the click of the society matron's heels, and then silence. She lifted her head. There was no point in waiting for Bebe's return when she needed something to drink far stronger than water.

She wondered if the bar had already been set up and rose to her feet. Closing the door behind her, she wandered toward the gardens.

Paige didn't see Zoe, but everything else was there, the subtle yet elegant touches she'd provided, the fairy lights, the classy tables with glowing centerpieces, and the dance floor. Drawing a deep breath, Paige looked around and realized this was more than a business loss to her.

For the first time in her career, she had chosen everything herself. She'd organized it all not to suit Hilde, but to suit herself, as though planning the wedding she'd never have.

And here it was. The setting sun, the gentle ocean breezes, the mingled scents of sea and flowers, and the gorgeous gardens all provided the perfect location, one Paige could never have imagined. And everything else, from the place settings to the menus to the music, struck a chord.

As if that thought had conjured a tune, Paige heard the low sound of strings beginning to play "It Had to Be You" and her throat filled up. It was silly, really...

What? Why were they playing so early? Paige turned, ready to find out, only to see Siegfried standing before her, looking totally gorgeous in his tux.

"There you are," he said. "I've been trying to reach you for days."

Paige attempted to speak, but nothing came out. Here and now, in this perfect setting, with the last rays of the sun striking his dark hair, Good-looking Guy had never looked better. It was as if a prince had stepped out of a dream to complete her fantasy.

"I've been wanting to ask you something, and now seems the ideal opportunity," he said, lifting a hand to take in their surroundings. And then, to her complete astonishment, he got down on one knee.

Paige's first thought was to help him up. Had he twisted his ankle? Was there something wrong with the new flagstones?

But when she reached for him, Siegfried held out something that sparkled. Although the fairy lights blinked in the nearby bushes, their glow wasn't reflected in any glittering decor or champagne flute. It was a diamond ring that was staring her in the face.

"Paige Porter, will you marry me?"

Paige wondered if she'd already hit the bar and had so many drinks she was hallucinating. Or maybe she'd slumped over her keyboard again, and this whole scene was some kind of delusion brought on by lack of sleep and heartbreak.

But she blinked and pinched herself, and Siegfried was still there, looking up at her with those guileless brown eyes. They were beginning to fill with anxiety, and fixer that she was, Paige wanted to remove any shadows from them, now and forever.

So just like that, she dismissed all her reservations and long-held beliefs and leapt right into the fairy tale.

"Yes," she said. The heart she had guarded so long began singing, or was that the music, which seemed to swell in answer to her reply?

All Paige knew was that Siegfried slipped the ring on her finger and took her in his arms. And he was still the best kisser and the best guy she'd ever known. In fact, she was eager for another demonstration of just how good he was with his hands.

But through her romantic haze, Paige heard the sound of a throat clearing, which brought her back to reality. Or at least she realized they were making out in the wedding venue, where the guests would be arriving any minute.

The wedding... Paige had to consult with Zoe and Bebe on what they were going to do. She turned around, back in business mode, but Bebe was standing right there.

"You'll have to hurry," the society matron said.

"To do what?"

"Why, to get ready, of course."

Paige was in such a daze that she let the older woman lead her into the house and her office suite. But when she saw Hilde's wedding dress laid out, she let out a squeal. "Are they back?"

"Oh no, dear," Bebe said. "The gown is for you."

"I can't fit into it," Paige said.

"Why not? It should be your size. When I saw it, I knew it would be perfect for you, so I ordered one just in case. You never know how long these creations are going to be available, you know."

Setting aside the fact that these creations were enormously expensive and hard to come by, Paige blinked in confusion. "You want me to marry Siegfried now? Today?"

"Of course, we don't have the proper licenses to satisfy the legalities, but you can take care of those later," Bebe said, waving her hand airily. "After all, it would be a shame to let all your beautiful planning go to waste."

Paige shook her head, then laughed, then reached for her wedding gown. She couldn't imagine what the guests would think, but she supposed everyone was used to the foibles of San Francisco's most eccentric family. And she knew very well what Zoe would say.

Bibbidi bobbidi boo.

ABOUT THE AUTHOR

Deborah Simmons began her writing career as a journalist, but left non-fiction for the world of happily ever afters. She's the author of twenty-eight novels and novellas published by Avon, Harlequin, and Berkley, as well as an indie romantic comedy. Among them are a USA Today Bestselling anthology and her popular series on the medieval de Burgh family.

Her books *A Lady of Distinction* and *The Gentleman Thief* were finalists for Romance Writers of America's annual RITA competition. And two other releases, *The Gentleman's Quest* and *Glory the Rake*, were up for The Daphne du Maurier Award of Excellence for Mystery/Suspense. Her work has been translated and published in more than thirty countries, with graphic novel editions available in Japanese.

DeborahSimmons.com
Facebook.com/authorDeborahSimmons

WORKS BY DEBORAH SIMMONS

www.ingramcontent.com/pod-product-compliance
Lightning Source LLC
Chambersburg PA
CBHW060927180626
46817CB00004B/1425